Pibby's
ADVENTURES

KEITH MOCK

Copyright © 2024 Keith Mock
All rights reserved
First Edition

PAGE PUBLISHING
Conneaut Lake, PA

First originally published by Page Publishing 2024

ISBN 979-8-89157-392-5 (pbk)
ISBN 979-8-89157-426-7 (digital)

Printed in the United States of America

INTRODUCTION

Sit back and let me take you back to my childhood experience. I grew up in a relatively poor family. We didn't have a whole lot, but we had enough. My brother and I didn't have all the toys other kids had, so we made up all our toys, such as crushed beer cans as baseballs and tobacco barn sticks as bats. We played a game of baseball with them. If we could smack that can on top of our grandpa's house, it was a home run. I bet we played for hours on end.

Our grandparents lived on a small farm in a town called Rocky Ford in South Georgia. My grandparents didn't have much, but it seemed like paradise to two boys, eight and ten years old. I tell ya, there ain't much my brother Tracy and I didn't get into those summers at Papa and Grannie Mae's house. We were daredevils to say the least. Looking back, I know the good Lord was a looking out over us two.

I think back to a certain summer day. We both woke up early. Well, you had to at Papa's house. He got up with the chickens. You would smell coffee brewing and bacon cooking. Are you starting to see why this was heaven to us?

My papa had gotten into a hunting accident earlier in his life and lost his leg from the knee down, so he didn't farm much anymore, just mainly kept pretty good-sized garden full of butter beans and such. Papa had to quit school early to help his family on the farm. He couldn't read or write, but you couldn't tell it by the way he handled himself.

My granny Mae was about five feet tall and spunky as a rattlesnake. She had to work to make ends meet around the farm. Granny worked at Dairy Queen my whole childhood. I remember she'd get off at closing time and my brother and I would be waiting at the back door to get all the leftovers she brought home. Her freezer was always full of Dilly Bars and parfaits. Heaven, I tell ya! Granny knew my favorite food was butter beans, and she made sure she cooked them every meal it seemed.

Well, getting back to our story. It was a pretty normal day till we decided we were gonna conquer the giant pine tree in the back cow pasture. Now we've conquered the lower limbs a long time ago. This day was gonna be different.

"I bet I can climb higher than you can," Tracy said.

You know what is about to happen, but I'll tell you anyway. The dare was on. We proceeded to climb higher and higher. Now Tracy was known to fall out of everything he ever climbed. Heck, Mom said he even fell out of the baby bed when he was a baby. The boy was no squirrel.

So we were about to the top of this giant pine tree. I was a little behind him, and all of sudden, I heard branches breaking limbs falling and my brother passing me on the way down, feet last. I was sure he was dead, so I made my way back down to find him sitting straight up on his butt, smiling. Needless to say, we never told anyone how the tree kicked our butts that day.

The very next day, we were riding small pine trees down to the ground. Okay, we had short memories. You see, you would shimmy up a small pine tree to the top, kick your legs out, and ride it to the ground. Well, you guessed it, Mr. Tree Master did it again. So he shimmied up this tree, kicked his legs out, and I heard a loud *pop*. The treetop broke off, and Tracy came falling straight to the ground. We laughed our butts off all day about it. Heaven.

We would do crazy stuff like that all the time. There was this one summer different than the rest. I remember sleeping in this feather bed. You would sink so far down in it, you would barely be able to move. I'd lay there and look out into Papa's pecan grove and watch the squirrels and all the other animals run all over the trees and grove. Now this is where it gets strange, so hold onto your britches. You're not gonna believe the story I'm gonna tell ya. It was a day just like all the rest. I was lying in bed, smelling coffee brewing, bacon cooking, and my granny was giving my papa a to-do list before she left for work. I turned over and began to watch all the squirrels gathering pecans and running back up the pecan trees. I drifted off to sleep watching them, and this was where my adventure began. Hold on!

CHAPTER 1

Squeaky

I woke up shivering and felt really weak. Where was I? And why was this tree I was beside with so dang big? I thought to roll over and go back to sleep, but I was no longer in my bed. I was outside on the ground. I stood up and looked back at Papa's house, and it was huge! Everything was huge! There was a Mr. Pibb can beside the tree, and it was the size as me! What was going on here? I've got to be dreaming, so I went and pinch myself. Fur! What the heck?

About that time, a giant squirrel with pants on came running at me, screaming, "Sova! Sova!" and grabbed my hand, no…paw! What? He pulled me up a pecan tree and ducked in the first hole he saw. "Are you crazy?" he said in a squeaky kinda voice. "Why are standing out there with Sova on patrol? And why are you naked?"

"Naked?" I asked.

"You have no clothes on," he squeaked back.

Suddenly, I felt the urge to cover myself, so I ran behind a pile of pecans that were piled in the corner. "Where am I?"

"Why you're in the grove," he squeaked again.

"What am I?"

"That's a silly question. You're a squirrel, dummy."

"Squirrel! I'm not a squirrel. I'm a boy, and I live in that giant house over there."

"Well, you sure look like a squirrel to me," he said. "Never saw a human with a tail like that." He giggled. "Plus, you climbed this tree pretty fast for a boy. What's wrong? Did a pecan fall and hit you in the head?"

"No!" I said. "I'm a boy!"

"Okay! Okay!" he said. "Let's try introducing ourselves first. I am Squeaky."

Well, that figures, I thought to myself.

"What's your name?"

"My name is Keith."

"Whoa! That's gotta be a human name. I've never heard of that before," Squeaky said.

"Well, that's my name," I said. "I don't know what's going on here, but you wouldn't happen to have some pants, would you? I feel a draft over here."

Squeaky said, "Stay here. I'll run over to my hole and grab some."

"Wait! What about this Sova thing?"

"Oh, he ain't as fast as me," he said, smiling. Squeaky disappeared out of the hole in a flash.

I was thinking, *This is a crazy dream but a very cool dream. Think I'll roll with it. What the heck.* I started checking my new body out, long bushy tail, little fingers and toes, not too bad. Squeaky said I had a human name, so I better find another one. About that time, I thought about that huge Mr. Pibb can at the bottom of this tree. Pibb…Pibby…Mr. Pibb? I'd go with Pibby. It sounded good.

Squeaky came hauling his butt back in the hole with a pair of overalls and a white shirt.

I said, "When did squirrels start wearing clothes anyway?"

"Why do humans walk around naked?" he asked.

Just roll with it, I said to myself. "Never mind, thanks for the clothes, man. So how did you get your name? Not that I didn't already know but thought I'd ask anyway."

He said, "My grandpa gave it to me."

That instantly made me think of my papa. *Am I still asleep, or no way I'm really here? No way. Did he come in to wake me up?* Well, he would usually let us sleep as long as we wanted to, so that was probably it.

PIBBY'S ADVENTURES

"I think I need to change my name if I'm gonna fit in here. Squeaky, what do you think about Pibby?"

"Sounds good," Squeaky answered. "Well, if you're gonna stay here long, I need to tell you a few things." So he started his list. "First and most important, Sova, always be on alert for him."

"What is he?"

"He can soar over the grove and dive with great speed, swoop away with you in a second."

"Oh, he must be an owl," I said.

What's an o…w…l?" Squeaky said in a confused tone.

"Well, it's a bird that eats squirrels like you," I smarted back. He got real quiet and turned away from me with his head down. "What is it, Squeaky?"

"My mom got taken away last winter while trying to warn me Sova was in the grove."

"I'm sorry, man. I didn't mean it to be mean." That was when I realized this was like a real life but a dream? "Go on, Squeaky, what else do I need to know?"

"Well, you better tell them you fell in the creek and you washed out here from another grove or patch of woods 'cause they don't usually let animals walked from our grove in here," he said with serious look on his face,

"They?" I asked.

"The three guardians of the grove. They're giants, twice as big as us and different colors."

"Of fox squirrels," I said.

"They're not foxes, they're squirrels. That pecan must have really hit you hard." He laughed.

"No, we call them fox squirrels 'cause, well, I don't really know why, but that's what we call 'em."

"Well, that's stupid calling a squirrel a fox." He sighed. "First place we better go is to the guardians," he said. "No, let's talk to Mudar first to get his advice."

"Mudar, who the heck is that?" I asked.

"He's the oldest animal in the grove. He lives in a hole at the very back of the grove."

3

"Let's go."

"No, not now!" Squeaky shouted. "Sova is still in the grove."

In my mind, I was not worried 'cause this was just a dream, and I couldn't really get eaten by an owl in a dream, but like I said before, roll with it.

"We'll head out in the morning," Squeaky said.

"Won't your dad miss you tonight?" I was hoping his dad was still around after I had said it.

"He knows if Sova is around, I'm gonna stay put till he's gone. We're taught that at a very young age."

I could tell it was getting late by the light coming through the hole, so I curled up the way I saw Squeaky do and closed my eyes, thinking, *What a crazy dream.*

Squeaky said, "Good night, Pibby. I think you'll like it here once you meet everyone."

"Good night, Squeaky." *Please don't wake me up yet. I wanna see where this dream takes me*, I said to myself as I drifted off to sleep.

*****

"Wake up!"

I jumped up to my feet, all four of them now, and said, "Dang, you scared the crap out of me, Squeaky."

"Sorry," he said, "but if we want to catch Mr. Mudar aboveground, we've gotta go."

"Aboveground?" I asked.

"Yeah, he doesn't come up much," Squeaky said.

"How 'bout Sova?" I asked.

"He only comes out right before dark most days," he said with hope in his eyes.

"Okay, I'm ready." Or at least I thought I was.

Squeaky left the hole first, then I poked my head out. *Whoa, look how big this place is!* The trees looked like skyscrapers, and the grove looked like giant city made of trees. I was in awe. Meanwhile, Squeaky was already on the ground, looking up at me.

"Come on, Pibby, we gotta move."

PIBBY'S ADVENTURES

"I'm coming, kinda new to this tree climbing thing," I said. I took one step, then two—hey, I got this—as I was falling through the limbs, hitting everyone on the way to the ground.

When I finally hit the ground, Squeaky came up, laughing. "You okay?"

I said, "If only Tracy could've seen that!"

Squeaky asked, "Who?"

"Never mind," I said.

"Follow me and don't forget you accidentally got washed up in this grove."

"Okay, I heard you the first time."

So off we go. It wasn't long before we came upon a squirrel dressed in jeans and had a tool belt on with tools I've never seen before. They looked like drill bits but real fat on the end of them.

"Hello, Mr. Timmerman, are you building hole homes in this tree today?" Squeaky asked.

"Yes, sir," he said. "The grove is getting crowded these days with all you children growing up. I've four new homes this year already. Who's this youngster you have with you, Squeaky? Don't recall seeing him around here."

"No, sir, he got washed up by the creek yesterday."

"You better take him to see the guardians as soon as you can," Mr. Timmerman said in a firm voice.

"Yes, sir, we're going to see Mr. Mudar first."

"Okay, run along. I got work to do."

So we're off again. I never knew I could run so fast. Man, this was awesome!

Squeaky looked back and said, "We've got to take the trees to get where Mr. Mudar lives. You up to it?" He laughed out loud.

"You just show me, tree funny man squirrel, whatever you are." Before I knew it, he was halfway up this huge tree, looking back at me. "I'm coming, I'm coming." I jumped as hard as I could and stuck to the tree like glue. *Hey, this is awesome!* I went up that tree with no effort at all. Before I knew it, I was at the top with Squeaky. Then I looked down. Whoa, I never imagine it would look that far down.

5

Squeaky said, "Now all we have to do is jump to these three trees, and we'll be at Mr. Mudar's hole. Jump!"

"You are crazy as a bedbug if you think I'm jumping!"

"Nothing to it, just jump high, and you'll eventually hit a limb and hang on," he said with beaming confidence. "Watch me!" he screamed as he was falling through the air.

I can't die. I'm in a dream, I kept repeating to myself. So off I went and jumped as hard as I could while waiting to hit a limb to grab on. Problem was, I never hit a limb, so when I hit the ground and bounced three times, I looked up at Squeaky and said, "What the heck?"

He screamed, "You got to jump toward the tree, dummy!"

So back to the tree, I went. I crawled out to the end of the limb and off I went again. Only this time, I jumped toward the tree. I grabbed the first limb I hit and held on for dear life. "I did it!" I screamed out loud.

"Okay, only two more to go, Pibby," Squeaky said while laughing.

We finally made it to the bottom of the last tree, and Squeaky said, "Mr. Mudar lives in that hole over there."

"Mr. Mudar, are you home?" Squeaky said in a loud voice. "Mr. Mudar!"

"Okay, okay, I'm coming up!" a voice from the hole said. In what seemed like an eternity, he finally showed up. He was a large old turtle with old hat and scarf around his neck. I could tell he had been around for a long time.

"What is so important, Squeaky?"

"I've got a friend I want you to meet and give some advice to. This is Pibby."

"Nice to meet you, sir," I said as polite as I possibly could.

"Well, let me look at you, boy. You're not from this grove, are you, son?"

"No, sir, I got wash up here in the creek yesterday."

"So what grove are you from, boy?"

I was at loss for words, so I blurted out the truth as I knew it, "I was a boy. Now I'm a squirrel and have no idea how this happen!"

He stared at me for a minute and looked at Squeaky and said, "He must have hit his head on a rock in that creek." Squeaky was shaking his head yes! "Well, you know you've got to take him to the guardians, but I'd leave that boy story in your head, Pibby, if I was you."

"Yes, sir, I will."

"Y'all can stay for a while if you wish. I've got some fresh corn and carrots down here if you wish to eat with me."

"Yes, sir!" we both said aloud.

As we were walking down the hole, I said, "Do you have any butter beans?" They both looked at me with a strange look on their face. "Just thought I'd ask," I said with smirk on my face.

When we got to the end of the hole, it was hallowed out into four or five big rooms. We made our way to the kitchen, and there was an assortment of all kinds of nuts and vegetables. We took a seat at his table carved out of the hard rock the hole was made of.

Mr. Mudar replied, "I've lived here for nearly a 150 years now and raised many animals in my lifetime."

Squeaky and Mr. Mudar grabbed some carrots and nuts and just started eating while me... I was new at this, so I just watched them and did what they did. We ate until our bellies couldn't be stretched anymore.

After we were finished, Mr. Mudar said, "Let's go to the pool and relax for a while."

I asked, "Pool?"

"Follow me, gents," Mr. Mudar said in a braggadocian way.

We followed him to the back of his hole home, and it opened up to a large pond, well, like a goldfish pond sort of. It had rocks, lily pad flowers, and a spring that bubbled in the middle. You could tell he was proud of what he built here.

"Jump in!" he shouted.

Squeaky hit it first, and I was soon after. Man, I bet we stayed in there for hours on end. Mr. Mudar just sat in the water's edge and laughed at us all day long. After a day of fun in Mr. Mudar's pool, we headed back to the kitchen and dried off and ate some more. We sat around the table, listening to Mr. Mudar's stories of how he escaped death several times before he settled here in his hole home.

"Y'all better stay here tonight for I'm sure Sova is on the prowl by now. You can each pick a room to stay in, and I'll wake you up good and early so you can make your way to see the guardians."

Lying there in bed later, I drifted off to sleep, thinking, *Man, what a dream.*

CHAPTER 2

The Guardians

"Get up, boys!" Mr. Mudar said in stern but nice way.

I rolled over and looked at my furry hands, paws, whatever you wanna call 'em, and thought, *Still here!*

"Okay, boys, let's get you fed and on your way. It'll take you awhile to get there."

We ate till our bellies were full and said our goodbyes, and off we went. Squeaky led, and I followed for a while, then came to an opening where there were no trees at all.

"What happened here?"

"There was a big storm that came through and took a lot of trees and hole homes at the same time," Squeaky said, looking down. "We've got to be careful crossing this 'cause we'll be out in the opening with no escape trees. Stay close to me and don't look back."

We started running and sneaking across the field when all of sudden, Squeaky started screaming, "Run, Pibby, run toward the trees!"

I looked across the field and saw a reddish-gray figure running toward us. *Fox!* I knew what foxes do to squirrels. We ran as fast as our feet could carry us, but he was gonna cut us off before we could reach the trees. He cut us off about ten feet from the edge of trees, and we came to a dead stop in front of him.

"Well, well, what do we have here?" he said with his teeth glaring at us. "I can only catch one of you, so which will it be?"

Squeaky had a face full of fear and had frozen solid in his tracks. I, on the other hand, was thinking, *It's a dream. I can't die in a dream.* "You're not gonna catch either of us. You're too fat and slow!" I said with scared confidence. "We're the fastest squirrels in the grove!"

"Hahaha, you're a brave little fellow, but I think I just made my mind on who I'm gonna eat."

All of sudden, he came my way. "Squeaky, get to the trees!" I screamed as loud as I could and took off back across the field. He was right on my tail, and I was thinking, *I hope this is a dream. I hope this is dream.*

All of sudden, he grabbed my tail and slung me across the field. Then he came back and grabbed me again and slung me the other way. If this was a dream, it sure wasn't fun anymore. I thought I was about to be eaten in my dream.

All of a sudden, he dropped me and ran off toward the woods and heard the loudest noise I'd ever heard. Dog! It was a dog. He came running by, not even bothering to look my way.

"Run! Run, Pibby," I could hear Squeaky from the trees. I stood up with pain in my back legs, but I still managed to make it to the edge of the trees. Squeaky helped me up to the tree to the first hole we came to. I lay down as far back as I could get in the hole and looked back at Squeaky.

"You okay?" he asked.

"I think so, but my leg hurts a little."

"Let me look at it. It's only a scratch, Pibby. You're so lucky," he exclaimed. "You saved my life, buddy. I thought we were both goners. No one gets away from Roka unless he lets you go. He has taken several animals from the grove. Let's stay in here for a while and make sure he's not around anymore," he said while looking out the hole.

I was still in shock, thinking, *You can't feel pain in a dream, can you?* A new level of fear entered my body as I thought about it. "Where does he live, Squeaky? Close?"

"No, you hardly ever hear of him being this far in the grove," he said, looking back over his shoulder.

"Let me rest for a while and be ready to go, okay?"

Squeaky said, "Take your time, buddy."

*****

"I'll get him next time," Roka said as he watched the dog run by. "They couldn't have made it far. He won't escape next time." Roka headed back their way.

*****

I dozed off a little while, and when I woke up, Squeaky was sitting beside me and asked, "You okay?"

"Yeah, I'm good. Let's go."

"We can't," he said. "He's back."

"I smell you, boys! Come down and play! Thought you were the fastest in the grove! Come on down!" Roka was laughing out loud.

"Don't make a noise. He'll leave eventually."

"I know he will," Squeaky said. Squeaky looked down from the hole, and Roka was lying at the bottom of the tree.

"I can wait all day, boys!" he said.

"What are we gonna do!" I said.

"Just wait," Squeaky said. We waited a little while, and Roka was not bulging.

"Trees, trees! Let's take the trees!" I said.

"Are you crazy? You're hurt, and face it, you're not the best at it! I can do it!" Squeaky went first. He jumped easily to the next tree and turned back and said, "Okay, you can do it!"

"Sure, try it," Roka said. "I'll be waiting if you don't make it."

I jumped as hard as I could and tried to grab the first limb but missed it. Luckily, I landed on the next big limb with a belly flop. The next two trees were easier, and it got better as we kept going.

Finally, Roka said, "Forget it, I'll get you next time," and disappeared into the bushes.

Finally, we shook Roka, and I said, "I'm tired. Squeaky, let's rest for a while."

"No use," he said. "We're here."

"Whoa! Those are the biggest trees I've ever seen!" In front of me were three of the biggest trees in the grove. "They live in these?" I said, gasping.

"Yep, this is the guardians' guardianship."

As we got closer, I could see that no animal could get up those trees. They were surrounded by thick briar bushes that went all the way around the trees. They had wrapped the briars about ten feet up the tree. You could only get up these trees by jumping from a nearby tree, and that didn't look possible for a normal squirrel. *Oh, but these are normal squirrels*, I thought to myself.

I noticed a spoon hanging near on one of the trees from a small rope. Squeaky picked up a rock that lay next to it and hit the spoon with it, making a loud *ding*! Out of the first hole, a large black squirrel with what looked like an armor on and a white patch on top of his head came out and looked down at us. The second hole was a gray one with same armor on and white patch in the same place. Third was a brown one, about the color of us with matching armor and patch.

The third one spoke first. "Son, where have you been?"

"Well, Dad, it's a long story," Squeaky said.

"What have I told you? You're not as big and strong as your brothers. You can't be just wandering about in the grove all alone."

Squeaky looked down at the ground and said, "I know, Dad, I'm not like you and my brothers. I shouldn't take chances."

"Dad! That's your dad," I blurted out. "You didn't tell me one of the guardians was your dad."

"Who is this one speaking without permission?" the gray guardian asked aloud.

"I'm Pibby! I got washed to this groove by the creek and apparently hit my head on a rock! Sorry!" I said smartly.

"Stop talking!" the black one shouted.

"What is your business here, Squeaky?" his dad asked.

"Well, Pibby, like he said, was washed here from another grove by the creek and thought I should bring him here to see you."

"Which grove does he come from?"

PIBBY'S ADVENTURES

"Well, I...he can't remember!" Squeaky shouted. "He hit his head on a rock and can't remember anything."

"Yeah, that's it," I said, rolling my eyes at Squeaky.

"We usually send strangers on their way that wander into the groove. Where would he go? He can't remember anything. You can't just make him leave. Come on, Dad, talk to them please!"

"Squeaky, rules are rules in the grove, you know this."

"I won't cause any problems. I'll do my share of whatever it is y'all do here," I said, pleading.

The black one spoke up and said, "Let us discuss this matter tonight."

"It's getting late. Squeaky, take him to our hole home. We'll have our answer tomorrow," his dad said.

"Okay, Dad," Squeaky said in disgust.

Squeaky and I headed to his home, and I looked at him. "Dude, you didn't tell me your dad was a guardian!"

"Yeah, I don't go around bragging about it."

"But it's gotta be sweet having a dad like that," I said.

"Kinda," Squeaky said, looking down.

"But how is your dad so big—"

"And I'm so small!" Squeaky interrupted. "All my brothers are gonna be as big as Dad, but it happens from time to time. I'm Mom's size. Dad treats me like I can't do the things my brothers do. He never gives me the important task he gives my brothers."

I could see Squeaky didn't wanna talk about it, so I just said, "You're the bravest and fastest squirrel I ever seen, buddy."

"Thanks, Pibby."

We entered his hole home and ate a little as we talked about tomorrow. "What am I gonna do if they make me leave?"

"Sometimes they give new animals a task to perform to prove their worth to the grove," Squeaky said hopingly.

"Task? Like what?"

"Like seeing if you can make it from end of the grove to the other without getting eaten."

"Without getting eaten!" I said shouting. "I don't like the sound of that."

13

"I'm kidding," Squeaky said laughing. "Let's get some sleep. I'm sure it'll be okay. Dad will help us out, I hope."

We both drifted off to sleep, tired from all the day's events. I woke up early already worrying about their decision today. I really wouldn't know where to go if they made me leave. *Okay, wake up now! This dream seems real*, I thought to myself.

"You ready, Pibby? Let's head down. They don't like waiting," Squeaky said, rolling his eyes.

We arrived at the trees, and the guardians were already sitting in their same spots as yesterday.

"We've decided. We have never asked anyone to do what we're gonna ask to you do to prove your worth to this groove, but it's come to our attention that a very important member of the grove has wondered out of the grove and was accidently taken in one of those machines to the city. We have knowledge that she has made it to the grove inside the city. She is very important to the black guardian for she is his daughter. Your task is to bring her back safely, and you'll be welcome to the grove."

"Dad! You can't ask him to do this. No one has ever made it to the city!" Squeaky shouted. "This is a death sentence! Not fair!"

"Squeaky, we have made our decision. This is the only way he can earn his worth. Now silence!" his dad shouted.

"I'll do it! I'll save her!" I said half-heartedly. "I just go to the city and bring her back. How hard can it be?"

"Impossible," Squeaky said with tears in his eyes.

"Very well, it's settled. Squeaky, get him a map and the provisions he'll need for his journey," his dad demanded.

"I'm going with him then!" Squeaky shouted.

"You will remain in the grove. This is final," his dad said angrily.

"Squeaky, I can do this. Just show me on the map where she is, and I'll bring her back."

Squeaky just shook his head and said, "Come on!"

We got back to his hole, and Squeaky started packing stuff into a cloth sack and mumbling stuff under his voice, "I'll show them."

He showed me on the map where to start and where the city was. "Man, that's a long way!" I said, scratching my head.

Squeaky started packing another cloth sack full of food and other stuff. "Whoa! I can't tote that much stuff. It'll slow me down." As I was saying this, I realized what his plans were. "Squeaky, your dad will kill you. You can't do it."

"I'll prove to him I'm as good as all my brothers." Squeaky threw me one sack and slung the other over his shoulder and said, "Let's go!"

CHAPTER 3

The Task

We were off. I had no clue what I was doing. Squeaky was on a mission to prove to his dad he was worthy of his praise. "Squeaky, you sure this is what you should do?"

"I'm tired of everyone looking down at poor little Squeaky. We can do this, Pibby," he said with a fire in his voice.

I wasn't as confident as he was. Heck, I almost got eaten by Roka just yesterday. *What a dream*, I thought to myself.

"The first leg of our journey is to make it to the back edge of the grove. That's full of danger in itself," Squeaky said.

"Then across open country and to the edge of the city, then go to the middle of the city, and hopefully find this daughter of the black guardian."

"It's quiet a task, buddy," he said.

We had been walking for a while when we came to the opening I almost got eaten in. "Oh no, I'm not trying that again, Squeaky."

Squeaky said, "We have no choice. We have to cross it to get to the back of the grove."

"Okay, I've got an idea. We can't outrun him or fight him, so let's trap him."

"How?" Squeaky laughed.

"See that little pine tree over there? Help me bend it over. Do you have any rope?"

"A little," he said.

PIBBY'S ADVENTURES

We climbed to the top of the little pine and kicked our feet out and rode it the ground. "Okay, tie the rope to the top of the tree and the other end to this root. Make a loop in it that he can step in."

"Okay, it's done," Squeaky said.

"Now all we need is some bait."

"Well, he really wants you, Pibby, so I nominate you!"

"Okay, I'll do it. I'll go up that tree and make some plenty noise to draw him in the clearing. I'll act hurt and see if he'll take the bait. Well, not take it hopefully," I said, wiping my brow.

Squeaky did I as I said, and nothing, no sign of Roka. "He's not around, Pibby. Let's just cross it.

"Okay," I said. "Come on down."

Then I heard that voice. "Well, well, well, it's the fastest squirrel in the grove, clearly not the smartest though," Roka said, laughing. "You want to get away this time, Pibby, is it?"

I was hoping Squeaky had notice what was happening and stayed in the tree, but I was wrong.

"I'm coming, Pibby, hold on," he said.

I had to make this happen fast before Squeaky made it to us, so I pretended to be injured and trying to run.

"I did make an impression on you last time, little Pibby," he said, laughing again. Then he leaped toward me with his teeth snarling, his foot landed directly in the loop. I pulled the root away, the tree sprung straight up, and the loop tighten on his leg and pulled him up, and he was hanging upside down, fifteen feet in the air.

"We did it. We did it," Squeaky said, pointing at Roka.

"Let me down, you little vermin! I'll tear you to pieces!" Roka screamed while dangling from the tree.

"Not today," I said. "We better go, Squeaky. I'm not sure how long that tree will hold him."

We ran as hard as we could for as long as we could. We came to a stream and filled our bellies and lay in the water for a while.

"That's the crazy thing I've ever seen, Pibby. Where did you learn that?"

I told him, "My brother and I used to do that all the time." And as soon as I said it, a sadness came over me. I missed him terribly.

"That was awesome! We showed his butt, didn't we?"

"Guess we did, Squeaky, guess we did."

Squeaky said, "Let's get across this creek. We've got to make it to the big trees so we'll be safe this evening."

So we made our way to the big trees and moved to the tops and jumped our way across the grove for a while.

"You wanna stop at Mr. Mudar's place and see if he'll feed us again?"

"Heck yeah!" I said.

We stopped at Mr. Mudar's place, and just like before, he offered us food and rest.

"Where you headed at, boys?" he asked.

We told him about the guardians' task that they gave me, and he couldn't believe they would put that on young squirrels like that. "Well," he said, "let me give you few things for your trip."

He loaded us up with food and supplies and said, "Hold on, one more thing." He came back with what looked like a needle with a handle on one end. "Use it wisely and carefully," he said, shaking his finger at me.

The needle had sheath in fit it, so I stuck it in my belt like a sword. "The city holds many more dangers than the grove, so be careful and hurry back…please," he said with caring eyes.

"Thanks, Mr. Mudar, we'll be back soon to play in your pond again," I said as we were headed out the door.

"I hope so, I hope so," he murmured.

We had about an hour before we needed to take cover for the night, so we hurried as fast as we could to the back of the grove. The edge of the grove was right before us, and we both looked at each other, saying, "This is it!"

"Let's sleep in this tree tonight and head out in the morning."

"Okay, Squeaky, I'm tired anyway."

Tomorrow would be the beginning of our journey outside the grove. We made us a bed out of moss and fell asleep, thinking, *Wonder if Roka is still hanging in that tree?* laughing ourselves to sleep.

I woke up before Squeaky and had this feeling we weren't alone. When I turned around, the black guardian was sitting behind us.

Squeaky woke up and shouted, "How did you get in here without us hearing you?"

"If you are to be successful in this task, you must sleep lightly and always be on guard, or you will not survive," he said sternly. "I have been following you since you left, but I cannot go any farther. I must guard the grove for it is my sworn duty."

"Can I ask you something? Why me? I'm not anything special, but you chose me to save your daughter."

"You are special, Pibby. We all knew it as soon as we saw you."

"How?" I said.

"You have been human in the past. You will know the ways and habits as you travel through the city."

"What! So is this all real?"

"Yes, it happened once before, and I made her my wife years ago."

"What happened to her?"

"She just vanished one day, like she was never there. That's why finding my daughter is so important to me, you see?"

I couldn't wrap my head around what he told me, but I thought I knew it all along. "Mr. Guardian, I promise I'll do my best to bring your daughter back."

"Solace is her name," he said. "You must leave now. Squeaky's dad is looking for him."

"Okay."

We climbed down the tree, took one step, and we were out of the grove.

CHAPTER 4

The Forest

The land was dotted with trees, pastures, and a few farms here and there. I thought, *Not many trees to escape to.* Squeaky set a pretty fast pace to follow.

"Slow down, buddy, we have a long way to go!" I said, grabbing his shoulder.

"I know," he said. "I just wanna get close to that tree line for safety."

"Not a bad idea!" I said.

"We could see a farm up ahead away," Squeaky said. "Let's see if they have a garden or something. We can grab a meal on the way through."

We came to the edge of garden and saw some peanuts turn up ready for picking and grabbed a few. I saw Squeaky keep shoving them in his mouth. "What are you doing!" He turned around, and his cheeks were jammed full, laughing. I asked, "Are you starving, son?"

"Store them for later, try it."

"Okay!" I went to cramming them in. "It's amazing how many I can put in here!" I mumbled. "Sweet! I like it."

"Let's get out of here. Farmers don't take too kindly to us eating their crops."

We walked and talked for hours till we heard a voice said, "Hello!"

PIBBY'S ADVENTURES

I said, "Hello? Who is there?"

Then this rabbit stepped out of the bushes. He was wearing green shorts and a T-shirt. "Well, howdy!" he said, waving his hand.

"It's nice to see others animals. It's been awhile. I'm Pibby. This is Squeaky. We're headed to the city to find someone."

"That is a long way from here, guys. This someone must be something special."

I nodded and said, "Never met her. What's your name, sir?"

"Lapin, I live at the farm you just passed by. I've got plenty food at my hole home down by the farm if you're in need," he said.

"We have plenty food, and our jaws are slam full still," I said, laughing.

"I'll walk with you to the end of this place, if it's okay with you, fellows?"

"Sure," Squeaky said. "Can't wait. We gotta get on our way though."

"Let's go then," Lapin said.

"Lapin, you have any family?" Pibby asked.

"I had, a few years back, but they're grown and gone," he said sadly. "Oh, to be young again and go on adventures like you two! I have to warn you though, Sova! He lives in the next head of woods, and no animal is safe in there."

"Sova?" I asked.

"Yes, he has been living in there all his life. He comes out to feed right before dark and stays in there during the day. It's really thick and dark in there," he said, shaking his head.

"If we go around, how long will it take?" I asked.

"You can't because the big cement roads are on both sides, and you know, it's too wide to cross. You must go through the forest," Lapin said. "Well, I can't go any farther. The forest is right over that hill. Good luck to ya, boys! I'll have dinner waiting on your way back through."

"Thanks, Mr. Lapin. I hope to see you soon," I said as he turned away from us and headed home.

As we stepped inside the forest, we looked at each other with a fear running through our veins. It was so dark in here, and it was early afternoon. "That's crazy!" we both said at the same time. We pushed on for a while till we heard a loud screech, and we both said at the same time, "Sova!"

"Do I see someone brave enough to enter my forest?" Sova screeched in a loud screeching voice. "Surely they must be lost! Let's see who these brave souls are!" Sova swooped down and landed on a couple trees from us. "Who is that hiding behind the trees? I dare you enter my forest!" Sova said.

"We've got to pass through please! We won't stop. We'll go right through!" I shouted from behind the tree. About that time, Squeaky pointed to a hole right above us and motioned to head to it. I shook my head yes and slowly moved toward it.

"I could let you pass, but then again, I could eat you. I've made up my mind, I'll eat you!" Then he swooped down and barely missed us as we dove inside the hole.

"Whew! That was close!" Squeaky screeched. We ran to the back of the hole and sat down, shaking.

"You'll never make it out alive! Have a nice sleep, boys. I'll see you in the morning!" Sova said, flying off.

"What are we gonna do now, Pibby? We're stuck here. We'll never make it out alive!" Squeaky said with tears in his eyes.

"Let me think for a minute. You remember what Mr. Lapin said? Sova leaves the forest at night to hunt and comes back during the day," I said, walking in circles. "We got to travel at night!"

"At night!" Squeaky said.

"It's the only way. Rest, and when it gets dark, we leave." I was thinking to myself, *What if he doesn't leave? What choice do we have?* We gotta try.

It was almost dark, so we eased out the hole and to the ground. The moon was full, so we had good light to see the way. No sign of Sova, so we hurried as fast we could without making any noise.

"I can't tell if we're almost out or not," Squeaky said.

"Just keep moving! We've got to get there sooner or later." We walked and walked all night long, and finally, we couldn't go any longer.

"Let's find a place to rest, Squeaky." We found a tree hole to climb in and settle down.

PIBBY'S ADVENTURES

"We don't know where we are, Pibby! I've completely lost track in the dark," Squeaky said.

"It's okay, we'll pick it back up in the morning."

"But Sova will return in the morning," he said nervously.

"We'll figure it out after we get some rest, buddy. Let's eat something!" I said, rubbing my paws together.

We ate till we were full and settled in for the night. It had been a long tiresome night, and we were lost somewhere in Sova's forest.

"Let's just count our blessings. We're warm, and our bellies are full, and we're safe, Squeaky," I said.

"Yeah, I guess, Pibby." He sighed.

We both drifted off to sleep, not knowing what tomorrow was gonna bring. We woke up to Sova's voice outside our hole. "Have a nice sleep, boys? Y'all made a good way last night but not far enough! This is the end of the line. No one leaves my forest! I can wait you boys out. I ate good last night in the grove," Sova said, laughing. "I also picked your little rabbit friend up on the way back. I'll save him for later."

"Oh no! He's got Mr. Lapin," Squeaky said.

"You'll never get us! We can stay in here for a long time!" I shouted back at Sova.

"We'll see!" Sova answered.

Hours went by, and we could still see Sova right outside our hole. He had landed on a limb beside our hole. "What are we gonna do?" Squeaky asked.

"Let me think for a minute." Then I thought of the needle sword Mr. Mudar had given me. "We're gonna have to make a run for it! I'm gonna jab this sword in his back, and we'll make a run for it through the treetops."

"We'll never make it, Pibby! He's too fast!" Squeaky whispered.

"We can't stay here. He'll just wait us out. We can do this. As soon as I jab him, you jump to the first tree, and I'll jump to a different one. We'll meet up at the edge of the forest. We've got to be close. We can do it!" I was doubting myself as I was saying it.

"Okay, Pibby. If we don't make it, you've been a great friend to me since we met, thanks."

"You too, Squeaky, but we're gonna make it!" I said. "You ready?"

Squeaky shook his head. I pulled my needle sword, which was pretty long. I thought I've got to push in as far as I could. I eased up to the edge of the hole and moved out on the limb behind Sova and jabbed the sword as hard as I possibly could.

Sova made a loud screech and fell straight down toward the ground. "Go!" We both jumped to our trees and started jumping to the next one. I watched as Squeaky was doing the same in the tree next to me. I looked back. No Sova? What! Did I kill him? I stopped and yelled to Squeaky, "I think I killed him. I'm gonna check and see."

"Are you crazy?" Squeaky yelled.

"I wanna know." I jumped back a few trees to where he fell. He was on the ground jumping around. Apparently, the fall had broken his wing, and he couldn't fly. Squeaky came and sat beside me as we watched him attempt to fly.

"It'll be better shortly! I'll get you then!" Sova screamed in pain.

"Serves you right! You killed my mother!"

"She was delicious too!" Sova barked.

"I wanna finish it, Pibby!" Squeaky said with tears streaming from his eyes.

"He's finished already, Squeaky. He won't be able to eat or defend himself from anyone. He won't last long," I said with my paw on Squeaky's back. "Let's go, buddy."

We continued in the trees till we put distance between Sova and us. We moved to the ground and walked. Squeaky was quiet the whole way. I think his mind was on his mom. I heard sniffling a few times. I let him work through it on his own. Sometimes you just couldn't think of the right words to say.

A few hours later, we came to the edge of the forest and smiled and hugged each other. "We made it! I can't believe it! We made it!" Squeaky shouted.

"Sure did, buddy! Sure did." I couldn't believe it either, but there we were, standing outside the forest.

Screech! We heard Sova somewhere back in the forest. "Mr. Lapin!" We both shouted at the same time.

"Should we go back? Is it too late? What should we do, Pibby?"

"We've got to at least see, right?" I said, looking at Squeaky.

"Oh, I don't want to go back there, Pibby!"

"Then I'll go check. You find a place for us to stay when I return."

"Please come back, Pibby!" Squeaky answered as I stepped back into the forest.

I really didn't know where to even start, but I figured he'd be close to where it all happened with Sova. About an hour later, I could her Sova struggling to move about. I could tell he was really weak with his labored breathing. I went up a tree just above Sova's head and said, "Where is Mr. Lapin?"

"Probably dead by now!" he said.

"Please tell me! I want to help him."

"Why should I help you after what you've done to me? I will die on the ground. Do you know what a disgrace that will be to an owl like me?"

"What if I help you fix that wing? Will you tell me where he is?" I answered, thinking, *I must be crazy.*

"Fix my wing? How would you know something like that?"

I didn't bother telling him how I knew, but I had watched my papa do it to a bird that had flown into his window one day. He was a very softhearted man. "Don't worry about how I know but trust me, I can," I said, scared to death.

"You fix this wing, and I'll do anything you ask."

I climbed down and went just out of reach of Sova and said, "Okay, if I do this, first of all, don't eat me. Tell me where Mr. Lapin is, and you must let me and my friends pass back through your forest when we return this way."

"Okay, okay, just fix it already."

"Okay, I'll need two straight limbs, and I have some rope on my sack. We must set it back in place first, but it's gonna hurt!" I tied the rope to the end of his wing. He was so much more gruesome up close. I would sure not like to be eaten by him.

I ran the rope around the nearest tree and said, "Brace yourself, I'm gonna yank it back in place." I got a running start and pulled as hard as I could.

"Screeech!" Sova yelled in agony.

I grabbed the two sticks, put them on each side of his wing, and wrapped the rope around the two sticks and tied it off tightly. I moved back out of his reach and watched him while he wrenched in pain. He was really weak and sat beside the nearest tree.

"I'll do what you asked. Your friend is up that dead tree over there, lying in the very top. Forgive me if he's dead already," he said.

I climbed the tree as fast as I could, fearing the worst. As I cleared the top, I saw Mr. Lapin lying on his belly face down with deep scratches in his back. "Oh no!" I said as I rolled him over.

"Well, hey, ole boy! Fancy seeing you again. Got myself in quite a pickle here, haven't I?"

"Mr. Lapin? I was sure you were a goner."

"Just playing a little possum, hoping he forgot me here."

I helped him down the tree and on to the ground. "Pibby, it's Sova!" Mr. Lapin yelled as he pointed at Sova.

"He's harmless right now. He's badly wounded."

About that time, Sova yelled, "Come here, boy!" I came up to him. "One more favor? Will you please pull this out of my butt?"

I looked at it, and my sword was still protruding from his backside. I grabbed it, gave it a big yank, and out it came.

"Whoa! That feels better," Sova said in relief.

"Now you remember our promise!" I yelled.

"I will, I will."

"Let's go, Mr. Lapin. We'll make it back to Squeaky."

We made our journey back to the edge of the forest after a slow, agonizing walk for Mr. Lapin. It was almost dark by that time, so I had to find Squeaky fast.

"Squeaky!" I yelled as loud as I could. No Squeaky.

"Let's make our way to those trees to find a place to stay tonight." Mr. Lapin and I settled down in hole that isn't too far off the ground because of his injuries. "Let's rest here." I thought to myself, *Where's Squeaky? Please let him be safe.*

CHAPTER 5

Where's Squeaky?

We woke up the next morning to the bright sunlight shining through the hole opening. First thing out of my mouth was "We've got to find Squeaky."

"I'm not going anywhere, Mr. Pibby. I'd only slow you down," Mr. Lapin said.

I laughed at the "Mr. Pibby."

"What are you laughing at?"

"Oh, nothing, just a memory," I said, laughing.

"Okay, you go look for Squeaky. I'll stay here and heal, then head back to my farm. My promise still stands. I'll have dinner waiting on your way back through. By the way, thanks for saving my life, Pibby," Mr. Lapin said while giving me a hug.

"Bye!" I said as I was walking out the door. I only had one thing on my mind, find Squeaky. *You don't think he thought I didn't make it and left on his own? That's exactly what he did!* I thought to myself.

I quickened my pace and headed across the field. I came to the edge of the field, and it turned to mud and water as far as I could see. *This is nice.* Then I saw a set of footprints in the mud. These gotta be Squeaky's. I could see the tracks a long way in front of me. I followed the tracks most of the day, stopping to rest a couple of times. *He can't be that far ahead of me*, I said to myself.

All of sudden, his tracks stopped. They were there, then gone. It was like he vanished in thin air. There were no trees close, so he couldn't have went up a tree. Then I saw a slivering mark right beside his tracks. *Oh no! That looks like a snake slide!*

I followed the marks to this big opening on the side of a hill. The marks went in the hole, and the hole went deep in the ground. *Poor Squeaky!* I sat down in front of the hole and put my head in my hands and tried to hold back the tears. *He can't be gone! I've gotta go and see!*

Without thinking, I pulled my sword and started down the hole. I walked for what seemed like forever. There were passages going left and right, but I stayed straight. *Surely this thing has an end to it. Light, I see light!*

I eased up to a room that was large enough to hold several snakes, and they were still there!

"Who did you leave to guard the entrance?" I heard one snake say.

"No one is guarding it, sir."

"Then get someone up there now!" the largest snake said.

"Yes, Shona! Right away."

I was guessing this Shona was the boss of this place. No sign of Squeaky anywhere. *I'll search around a little. They all seem to be in that large room together.* I went to the left and searched an open room with eggs everywhere. *I'm guessing this is where all the babies are hatched.* Then another room had bones scattered everywhere as far as I could see. *Please don't let any of these be Squeaky.*

Then I saw one room behind all the snakes with movement in the shadows coming from it. *I've gotta see what's in there.* I hid under a pile of shed snake skins and tried to think of a plan to get by them. Surely they would sleep sometime, so I waited and waited till I actually feel asleep.

Suddenly, I awaken, scared of not knowing where I was. Then I remembered, but they were all gone, not a single snake in the room. *What happened? They see me and get scared?* I laughed at myself. *Why not? I'm probably fixing to die anyway.*

I took off toward the room in the back, and as I walked in, I saw two animals, and one was Squeaky, but he wasn't moving. *Oh no! Squeaky!* I went over to him. He had been bit, but he was still breathing. They must do that till they'd get ready to eat them, so they'd have a warm meal. I tried to wake him up, but it wasn't working. I went over to the other little guy to see if he was breathing, but sadly, he wasn't. He must had been too small for the bite they gave him.

I went back to Squeaky and threw him over my shoulder. Getting out of here, now that was another story. I ran across the big room, which was still empty, then I took the passage to the right because I knew they guarded the main entrance. *Maybe this one will go out another way.*

"Get everyone in and have them meet in the room!" I heard Shona shout.

They were all coming back in! I took to running as fast as my feet would carry me. *Please let this be a way out!* Suddenly, I saw a light. It was a way out, but there was a huge drop-off that went straight down to the stream.

"He's gone!" I heard one of them shout.

"Find him!" Shona shouted.

So I grabbed a big piece of bark and put Squeaky on, then climbed on myself. Something told me this was a bad idea, but I pushed off with my feet, and off we went down the hill.

"There they are! Get them!" Shona shouted.

They were right on our tail, and just as they were about to grab me, I went airborne. We hit the stream with a big splash, and the current whipped us away.

When the water hit Squeaky's face, he came to be and said, "Where are we?"

"You are safe, ole buddy! I got ya!" I looked back to see if anyone was following, but we were clear of that place.

Now to get out of this stream, I saw a limb hanging over the water coming up, and I said, "Squeaky, we're gonna grab that limb up, okay?"

"Okay!"

We jumped at the same time and grabbed the limb and climbed up the tree and into the first hole we saw.

"I'm so glad to see you, buddy!" Squeaky said with a hug. "I don't know what happened. I was walking, and something hit me, and I went out."

"It was a snake. It bit you, then took you down its hole, and stored you for a meal later. They called their leader Shona."

"I don't remember any of that," Squeaky said, scratching his head. "So you saved me again? You've got a habit of doing that! Thanks, Pibby, you're a real friend."

We sat and talked for the rest of the day. I guess we were just glad to be alive. We managed to lose all our food during the escape, so that was our first task of the next morning. We found a walnut tree and some wild blueberries and filled our bellies once again.

Squeaky said, "I have no idea where we are, Pibby. I've lost the map and everything else. We've been headed toward the sun the whole time, so we'll keep going till we end up somewhere. Pibby? What about Mr. Lapin?"

"Oh, he should be fine with few scratches. He'll be headed back to his farm shortly."

"How did you do it?" Squeaky asked.

I didn't want to tell him that I made a deal with his mother's killer, so I just made a story up, and he believed it. I knew eventually I would have to tell him the truth but not today. With our bellies full and our barrens straight, we headed out. We followed the stream down till we could cross and started our path toward the sun, not knowing what awaits us.

After the last two days, it couldn't get any worse, or at least I thought. The day was pretty uneventful. We walked and talked till we heard some voices up ahead. I told Squeaky, "Let's go up in the trees and check it out."

We eased up to where the voices were coming from, and two squirrels dressed in what look like army uniforms were arguing over who was gonna stand guard tonight.

"I'm not gonna do it! I did it last night!" said the chubbier one.

"Well," said the other, "I'm too tired!"

They were both carrying swords and drew them on each other. I spoke up, "Whoa, guys, don't hurt each other!"

"Who are you, my good fellow?"

"My name is Pibby, and this is Squeaky. Just didn't want y'all to hurt each other."

"Oh! We're just rehearsing for a play for our camp tonight."

"What kind of camp?" I asked.

"Just nine or ten of us that live in the camp. I'm Sim, and this Lot," Sim said with a big smile. "You should meet everyone and eat with us."

"Well, I never turn down a good meal. We'll stop for a little while, but we must push on soon." We followed them to a small camp set up in the middle of some huge boulders. "Nice!" I said as we walked in.

Squeaky and I met everyone, and we ate carrots, nuts, and wouldn't you know it, raw butter beans. They put on a play, and everyone seemed so happy to see us.

"Where are y'all headed?" Sim asked.

"To the city to find someone," Squeaky answered.

"City? That's a three-day walk from here. It's not an easy terrain either. There's a pretty rough stretch of rocks and hills not too far from here. Just stay pointed at the sun, and you'll run right into the city. Be careful once you get there. It's rough on little animals like us."

"Thanks," I said, "for the tip. I think we can handle it after the last two days. We better be off. Thanks for the hospitality. We'll be seeing you."

We were off again. We had a little pep in our step after the meal, so we made good time.

Squeaky said, "I kinda miss home a little. How about you?"

"To tell you the truth, I haven't given it much thought. But it got me to thinking, wonder what my grandparents are thinking? Did I just vanish out of their lives? Am I dreaming or dead? What was Tracy thinking? I miss my little brother, Dad, Mom, everyone. Will I see them again?" Suddenly, I felt sadness come over me, and I sat down.

"I'm sorry, Pibby, I didn't mean to make you upset."

"It's okay. I just hadn't really let it sink in till now. I may never see my family again," I said, choking up.

"You'll always have family as long as I'm here."

"Same here, Squeaky. Let's get going."

We came to the edge of the boulders, and Sim was right; it was gonna be a rough go at it. So we picked the safest path we saw and started down with it. After going for a little while, we picked a spot to settle down for the night. We didn't like staying in the open, but we really had no choice. So we unrolled our sacks, made some makeshift beds, and fell fast asleep.

We woke up to a familiar voice. "No one escapes Shonta." Shonta was curled around us completely. He was a giant snake, as black as the night sky.

"I believe you stole something from me, little one," he said, looking dead at me.

"Let's us go please! We're trying to find someone and bring them back home," Squeaky said.

"Now why would I care about that?" Shonta said in a sharp voice. "I'm just looking for my next meal, and I believe I've found it. Who shall I eat first?"

"Pibby! Do something!"

I pulled my sword, but he whipped it away with his tail. I couldn't move as he tightened his coil around us.

"Guess I'll start with the brave one!" He turned my way and opened his mouth, and I closed my eyes, knowing this was the end.

All of a sudden, a rock came out of nowhere, hitting Shonta in the head, then another and still another. Then a whole barrage of rocks was pounding Shonta. It was Sim and his camp buddies. They were screaming and throwing rocks as hard as they could.

"Well," Shonta said, "looks like I'm gonna have a full meal tonight," as he slid toward Sim and his friends.

I couldn't let him hurt them, so I ran and picked up my sword. I found the highest rock over Shonta's head, then I jumped toward his head, driving the sword deep between his eyes. Shonta curled up real tight and let out a big sigh, and he stopped moving.

"You did it!" Sim screamed. "You killed Shonta!"

Squeaky walked up behind me and said, "That's the bravest thing I've ever seen."

Sim came running up and said, "Wow! You are the man! Squirrel!"

PIBBY'S ADVENTURES

"Pibby! Pibby! Pibby!" they all chanted.

"This guy has been after us for years. We never slept in peace."

I went over and pulled my sword out of Shonta's head, and he moved a little. I stabbed him two more times for good measure. "We better move on before his friends go to missing him."

"We'll help you get through the boulder field, then we'll head back to camp," Sim said.

"Thanks," I said, "we need all the help we can get to make through these rocks." They helped us through the rocks, then we hugged and said our goodbyes.

CHAPTER 6

Paradise

After we cleared the rocks, we kept looking behind to make sure Shonta's friends weren't following us. My heart was still racing after what happened. We came around the corner to the most beautiful valley we've ever seen.

"Oh my!" I said aloud. "This place is awesome."

We found a small waterfall and stood under it for a while. There were blueberries everywhere. Flowers were growing all around the falls. Butterflies were on every bush.

About that time, a racoon came to the falls. "Don't worry, guys, just came by to get a drink of water." And soon the whole place was full of different animals of all shapes and sizes, drinking water and laughing with each other. There were deer, possums, birds, turtles, and even a small alligator. All were just enjoying each other's company. Each one had a story to tell. Of course, Squeaky chimed in with our story so far. He didn't tell all the way through it, and they all finished the story for him.

You see, word had been getting around about what we've been through and the way we got out of them. "Y'all are heroes, man!" everyone was saying at once. "How y'all strung up Roka, crippled Sova, and killed Shonta—all this for the love of a princess."

"Whoa! Whoa! Love of a princess?" I asked sarcastically. "I've never seen this princess. Heck, I didn't even know she was a princess, much less be in love with her."

PIBBY'S ADVENTURES

"Well, that's the story, my friend. It's all over this side of the country, how you two had a big love affair and that she was kidnapped the night before your wedding."

"Oh my goodness!" Squeaky said. "Y'all have got this story all wrong. They were already married, and then she got kidnapped."

"Squeaky! Don't make it worse!" I said, laughing.

"Well, it doesn't matter if it's true or not. We love a good hero and a love story 'round here," the smiling racoon said.

I enjoyed spending time with all the animals at this beautiful place, whether the story was true or not. Squeaky and I stayed there all day, telling stories, although all mine were of me and my brother Tracy's adventures back at the farm. I wondered if I'd ever get to tell him about all my adventures as Pibby. I sure hope so. He would really love this.

We asked the crowd if we could spend the night in this beautiful valley, and every single one offered us to stay with them. Guess we were some kinda heroes to them. They treated us like royalty.

"Gonna be hard to leave this place, Squeaky," I said while lying back, crossing my legs.

"Sure is!" he said while stuffing his face with strawberries. "Mighty hard!"

We ended up staying on the bank right by the falls all night long with most of the crowd. It felt good to sleep without having to look over our back for a change. The next morning, we woke up to a flock of singing birds at the falls. I thought it was the most beautiful sound I'd ever heard.

"Squeaky, we better head out."

Before we could get everything packed up and ready to go, the rabbit came up and said to us, "I want to show y'all something if you have time."

"Sure, what's your name, bud?"

"Well, most of my friends call me TC, so you can call me that."

TC had an old sock hat, and his pants looked old and faded. He sported an old wifebeater T-shirt and boots.

"Follow me down this path, boys. I think you may be able to use this on your trip."

We rounded the corner, and he had an old workshop carved out of the side of the hill. TC went and picked up what looked like a bow and arrow from the workbench in the shop. "You think this might be of some use to you, boys?"

"Sweet!" Squeaky said.

"I've got a target set up over here behind the shop. Come try it out."

Squeaky grabbed it out his hands and pulled back the string and split the bull's-eye.

"Well, I think he's a natural," TC said aloud.

Squeaky shot at least ten times and split it every time.

"You are a natural Robin Hood!" I said.

"Robin who?" They both looked at me with question.

"Never mind. You're really good with that, Squeaky. Don't think I need to try."

"I got plenty of arrows carved out over here, take them with you."

"Thanks, TC!" Squeaky said.

"No problem, Squeaky. I'm glad to help the heroes from the grove," he said, laughing.

"We really must be off now. We're burning daylight." They both gave me a weird look.

Squeaky said, "He has a weird way of talking sometimes."

"Okay, okay, let's go, Squeaky. Bye, TC. We'll catch you on the way back through."

"Okay, good luck, boys!"

So we were off. We found the trail pretty easy, beautiful also. This place was as close to paradise as you could come. Squeaky was walking proud with his newly acquired weapon, ready for the world. As we came to the end of the valley, we looked back and said, "We have got to come back to this place!" We turned and left our little paradise.

"Heroes!" Squeaky said out loud.

"Not yet, little buddy, we still haven't saved this so-called princess. Why didn't you tell me she was some kind of princess?"

Squeaky said, "Solace is this spoiled rotten girl who has gotten whatever she's wanted all her life. She just happened to be the daughter of a guardian and human-turned squirrel so that makes her unique. They all act like she's gonna save the grove from destruction or something. Solace cares about one thing, herself."

"So why would you risk your neck for her?" I asked.

"I'm not. I'm risking it to save you, Pibby."

I admit, that choked me up a little. "Well, you are a great hero after all!" I said jokingly.

We laughed about the whole story the crowd had told us back at the falls. We walked for the rest of the day through twists and turns, mud and rocks. We came to the edge of a county road.

"We're getting close, ole buddy," I said.

Crossing these roads was gonna get worse and worse. I remembered seeing animals on the side of the road while riding with my parents, not a pretty sight. These roads weren't bad, hardly any vehicles at all. This was all new to Squeaky though. He had a new kinda fear in his eyes. "We got this, buddy!" I said to reassure him.

As we hurried across the road, we hit the trees as soon as we got to the other side. While sitting in the top of the highest tree we could find, we could see the city, still a ways away.

"We'll never make it today, but let's get as close as we can," I said.

On the outskirts of town, we came across more and more houses as we got closer.

"I'm starving!" Squeaky said, rubbing his chubby little belly.

"Let's find a bird feeder. There's got to be one in these backyards." I spotted one at this old house with flowers everywhere and a small birdbath underneath it. As we got closer, we could hear the birds.

"You've been here long enough. Let me on there."

"No, it's my turn. Move over!"

The birds we're fighting over the food and a spot to land on the feeder. We eased down the tree toward the feeder and got to the point where we could jump over.

"Don't you dare! This is not for squirrels! We barely have room for all of us!" the red bird said, looking our way.

"Well, you better move. We're coming in!" Squeaky and I jumped at the same time, knocking the feeder to the ground, busting wide open. There were sunflower seeds everywhere. We started gorging ourselves, filling our jaws in the process.

"Now see what you've done!" said the annoying red bird. "Now we have to put ourselves in danger while trying to eat."

"In danger from what?" Squeaky asked.

"Smokie!" the bird said.

"Who is Smokie?"

"The large gray cat that's sneaking up on you now."

We were up on the tree in a split second, and sure enough, Smokie, the cat, was creeping toward us.

"Whew! That's a big cat! He hadn't missed any meals lately, that's for sure," I said, laughing.

"That's she," Smokie said while licking her paws. "I'm Ms. Smokie. I rule this residence. I would very much like to eat one of you. Maybe the little chubby one?"

"That ain't gonna happen, Ms. Smokie!"

"If you hang around this residence long, I'll end up eating you. I've eaten just about every kinda bird there is. I really prefer squirrels. Y'all are a little meatier," Smokie said.

"Well, this is one chubby butt you won't be eating 'cause we're leaving!" Squeaky shouted.

We started up the tree.

"Come back when you can stay longer!"

We left Ms. Smokie with her birds and got back on track to the city.

"Do I look chubby to you, Pibby?"

"Not a bit!" I said, laughing.

CHAPTER 7

The City

I hadn't seen a human since I changed, so seeing this one was a new but frightening experience for me. She was in her backyard, just sitting in chair, sunbathing, I guess. I decided to go up to her and speak, not a great idea.

I said, "Hi, ma'am, my name is Pibby."

She screamed for her husband and said, "This squirrel has rabies and making noises at me. Get the gun!"

Now I knew what that meant, so I got the heck out of there. Once we were clear of danger, Squeaky asked, "What were you thinking?"

"Just trying to introduce myself to her," I said, not understanding.

"She's a human. All she sees is a squirrel, that's it. I can't explain it, but that's all they see. I'm sorry, Pibby," he said.

"I don't understand the 'two different worlds' thing, but I'll better learn it, or I won't see much of either for long."

We came to the first subdivision and kinda made our way through the backyards of this giant houses. Every once in a while, we'd run into these other squirrels and animals, and they would kinda nod and turn their heads. All the animals here were dressed different than us. They had more like uniforms on, kinda like what my granny would wear at DQ when she worked there.

We finally ran into someone who would speak to us, so we asked, "How far is the park in the city?"

The old-timer said, "About a day's walk that way," as he was pointing toward the sun. "What's so important at such a dangerous place? You can't just walk in there, you know. It's guarded by all the emperor's men."

"Who's the emperor?" Squeaky asked.

"He has ruled the park for years. He's a large version squirrel and very ruthless. It's probably guarded extra heavy for the wedding ceremony in five days."

"Whose wedding?" I asked.

"His, he's marrying a newfound princess. We heard she's from the countryside down east."

"Solace!" we both said at once.

"Yeah, that's her name, although we're told she's not too fond of the idea. The emperor is holding her captive in his so-called palace, which is really just an old city building they don't use anymore. You'll never get close to her, if that's who you come after. The emperor has many friends in the ground and in the sky, if you know what I mean," he said, shaking his head.

"Well, we'll see about that!" Squeaky said, lying his hand on his bow and arrow.

"Watch the humans around here. They don't like animals much, particularly squirrels. You won't get much help from any animals either. They've all lost family members to the emperor. Okay, I've got to get this food to my family. It's getting dark. Good luck on your task, you'll need it," he said.

"It is getting dark, Squeaky. Let's hold somewhere around here till morning."

We found an old hole in someone's toolshed and made do for the night.

"Pibby, it sounds like we're in above our heads with this one. I don't see us being able to free Solace from the emperor's so-called palace."

"We were over our heads with Roka and Sova and Shonta, but we found a way, didn't we?" I asked.

"Yeah, I guess, but, man, this may be too much for just us two."

"Just get some sleep, Squeaky. We'll work on a plan in the morning. I didn't know how, but I was gonna save the princess for her dad, the black guardian. Just how, I hadn't figure out yet."

*****

The sun woke us up early the next morning, and we had food on our mind. We left our little makeshift hole and headed out into neighborhood, not forgetting what the stranger had told us about the humans.

Boom! Boom! I heard the gun go off twice. Then I heard the bird shot sprinkle the trees around us. "Run, Squeaky! They're shooting at us!"

"Think you missed them, son," I heard the man say to his son.

"You okay, Squeaky?"

"I think so, I just got a pain in my ear," he said.

I looked and one of the bird shot had grazed his ear, and it had a little blood trickling down it.

"What is it?" he asked.

"Nothing," I said, "was just a scratch."

"Well, that didn't take long! Man, they really don't like us!"

"I see a pecan tree up ahead. Be careful and stay hidden till we make it to it."

The pecan tree was loaded with pecans, so we didn't have any problems getting our bellies full. We figured we'd travel by trees till we couldn't anymore. It seemed safer than the ground. We went through many neighborhoods and crossed many streets via power lines. I knew we only had five days till the wedding, so we had to get to this so-called palace.

We came to the center of the city, and there it was, not the palace but the DQ. I couldn't believe it. I hadn't been to it that often because Granny would bring goodies home to us when she got off work. I gotta go, see if I can spot her.

"Where we going, Pibby?"

"I gotta check something out for a minute."

We made our way across the street from the front walk-up window. There she was, all five-foot nothing of her. Tears instantly filled my eyes. Memories flooded my mind as I stared at her. My love for her had not faded a bit since my change.

"That's my grandma, Squeaky, the smallest woman in the front."

"Pibby, I told you how humans see us. It's totally different."

"I know, I wouldn't do that to her anyway. She's the sweetest woman I've ever known." I didn't know if this was the last time I'd ever see her, so I sat there for the longest time watching her.

After a while, we heard, *Caw! Caw!* Two crows dove at us, nearly knocking off the power lines into the street. We hurried across the street and scurried down the power pole to the nearest tree. The crows continued diving at our heads, trying to hit us.

"What is the problem?" I shouted.

They landed in the same tree we had found safety in. "You can't enter this area without the emperor's permission. You must go back to the direction you came from, or we'll drag you back," they threatened.

"We're not hurting anything or anyone by being here!" I shouted.

They dove at us again, and the one in the back suddenly crashed to the ground with an arrow through his head. The second crow turned toward town and was gone in a flash.

"Nice shot, Squeaky!"

Squeaky, proud of his accomplishment, said, "I'm tired of everyone picking on us! Enough is enough!"

I could only guess where the other one went. We better move and fast! We knew the emperor would have everyone in command looking for us now. The plan for a surprise attempt to save the princess was out the door.

We made it to a back alley in town and saw a little tubby squirrel wearing jeans, a black belt, and an old Italian-looking hat. Hoping he was friendly, I got his attention by whistling at him. "Hey, can we ask you some questions?"

"Sure, partners, how can I be a service to ya?" he asked in a New York kinda slang. He lit a cigarette while we got a little closer to him.

PIBBY'S ADVENTURES

"We're trying to find the emperor's palace. We're trying to locate a friend."

"No friend of the emperor is a friend of mine," he said angrily.

"Trust me, we're not friends. He just had two of his birds try to take us out," I said.

"In that case, I'd be glad to help you out. The palace is three blocks that way, but it's hard to get in with all the guards around it. Many have tried, only to lose their lives while trying. There is one way in, but no one has ever done it."

"How?" I asked.

"By water, the stream runs under the entire palace. He knows no one can hold their breath that long, so he doesn't even guard it. It's not possible, my friend. By the way, I'm Tonito, Tony for short."

"We're Squeaky and Pibby. Nice to meet you."

"Come on down, rest awhile. I'll draw you a map of the palace."

"Okay, we probably need to let things cool down out here for a while. Squeaky just took out one of his birds."

"Yeah, good idea," Tony said.

We followed Tonito down this drainpipe till it opened up into a large room. The other animals in the room stopped and stared at us.

"It's okay, they're with me. They are on some mission to steal the princess from our great emperor," Tony said sarcastically.

"Pibby!" they all said out loud.

"What? You've heard about our task also?"

They all said, "Yes, it's all over the city."

"Great!" I said. "There goes the surprise factor. I'm sure this great emperor knows we're coming also."

"That doesn't matter, Pibby. He'll never expect you to enter from the water," Tony said.

"I hope you're right, my friend," I said.

"Now!" Tony said, laughing. "What about this great love affair you have with the princess?"

"I've never even met her!" I said aloud. The whole place was laughing at me, including Squeaky. "Okay, okay, tell me about this water passage. How long will we be underwater?"

"I'd say eight or nine minutes, maybe ten, depending on how fast you swim."

"Eight to ten minutes! That's not possible for anyone!" I shouted. "Maybe a fish!"

"Exactly!" Tonito shouted.

"What are you saying?" I asked.

"We've got fish friends that are big enough to swallow you and take you inside the palace."

"So you want me to let this giant fish swallow us and take us upstream into the palace?"

"Now you're catching on!" Tonito said, laughing.

"How do I know this fish won't decide that we're a tasty meal and change his mind?"

"Well, you might wanna make good friends with him before you try this."

"Man! I tell you what, this so-called princess better be worth it!"

"She's not!" Squeaky chimed in.

"Let's eat. We'll plan it all after dinner."

We all ate and laughed about my great love affair with someone I've never met.

*****

"Let's get to the plan. We only have a couple of days till the wedding. The stream runs one block over from here. We'll put you y'all in there, and it's about five blocks to the palace. Pesco, that's your ride's name, will hold enough air for you inside till you reach the underside of the palace. It gets tricky from there. We really don't know for sure if there will be guard at the entrance point. I don't think there would be because he knows no one can hold their breath that long. If y'all get in without being noticed, she is being held in the farthest room to the east or right, if that helps."

"How do you know which room she's in?" I asked.

Luca spoke up. "I've seen her in there. I used to carry food to the palace. I would have to put it in the room right next to her. Let me tell you, she was a fireball. She was raising sand at them every chance she got. She's there, I guarantee it!" he said.

"Okay, if I'm gonna play Jonah, I'm gonna need to meet this Pesco."

"Who's Jonah?" they asked.

"Never mind, I'll tell ya later."

"Okay," Tonito said. "Let's go before it gets too late. The sky is dangerous around sunset."

"Oh, we know!" Squeaky spoke up.

Tonito, Squeaky, and I left out the back, peeking around every corner. We figured the emperor knew we had made it to town by now. He'd have all his animals on the lookout for us. We made it to the water's edge, and Tonito took his hands and hit the tree that grew at the water's edge three times.

"He'll be here shortly. Let me talk at first." All of a sudden, this huge fish stuck his head up, not far from us. "Pesco! It's good to see you, friend."

"What do you want, Tonito?" Pesco said in a grumpy voice.

"You remember the plan we talked about a few weeks ago. Well, the animals we were talking about doing it are here now. Are you still down with taking them to the palace?"

"Do you still plan on doing your side of the deal, Tonito?" Pesco asked.

"What was it? One hundred pounds of bread?"

"Two hundred, one hundred for each passenger."

"What do you need that much bread for?" I asked.

"To eat, I stay hungry all the time," Pesco said.

"We get you three hundred pounds, and you're gonna eat a pile of it before climbing in that giant piehole of yours, no offense."

"None taken." Pesco laughed. "Okay, I'll be here at this time two days from now to pick you guys up."

"Sounds good!" Tonito answered.

"Bye, Pibby, Squeaky. Nice to meet y'all finally." Pesco disappeared beneath the water.

"How does he know our names?" Squeaky asked.

"Oh, everyone knows you two, you're—"

KEITH MOCK

"Don't say it."

"Heroes!"

Squeaky rolled his eyes.

"Let's get back to the hideout. We've got some bread to deliver tomorrow."

Tonito showed us where we could crash for the night, and we unpacked our bedding and lay down, thinking about the task ahead. *Getting in may not be that hard. Getting out, now that's something we didn't talk about. She better be worth it,* I thought while falling asleep.

Early the next morning, we set out to find the bread we owe Pesco. We pried open these doors to this bakery, and in the back room was big bags of scrapping, the edges they would trim off the bread the baker would make for the people that came into his shop. I guess he saved it for farmers that have ponds and such to feed their fish. Now each bag weighed around fifty pounds, so I couldn't carry this to the water's edge.

Tonito said, "No worries, I have a friend that can. I'll be back!"

And off he went around the corner. A few minutes later, Tonito came up riding a huge dog, Saint Bernard to be exact.

"Hey, guys, this Columbo. His owners gave him that name. He said he would be honored to help Pibby and Squeaky."

"How did he know us? Never mind, I know…heroes again, right?" I said.

Columbo grabbed two sacks at a time and carried them to the water's edge. Three trips, he was done. Pesco came by, and Columbo laid the sacks on Pesco's back, and he started swimming away.

"Don't forget to eat a big supper and an even bigger breakfast in the morning before you come!" I said as everyone was laughing at me. "Hey, I don't know about you, but I don't wanna end up as fish poop tomorrow."

Tonito said, "While we got some time to kill, let me show you two something."

We snuck up to this big factory on the edge of the town right next to the stream. Tonito ran around the back of the building, and we followed him closely. It was a grain bin where farmers brought their corn to be processed.

46

PIBBY'S ADVENTURES

"Look at all the corn to be eaten on the ground!" Tonito said.

"Wow!" Squeaky shouted.

"I'll just load it in the back of my pickup," I heard a man say.

I knew that voice! Papa! It was my papa, and before I knew it, I ran over to him, saying, "Hey, Papa, I missed you so much!"

He said, "Hey, little fella, you fell out of your tree. Where's your mama?"

Then a man with a broom came up and started trying to swat me out of the building. "Dang, squirrels always in here eating the corn off the floor!"

"Well, squirrels gotta eat too, Ben," Papa said, laughing.

"Not my corn, they don't!" he said, knocking me outside the building.

Squeaky grabbed me by the arm and dragged me away. I looked back at Papa and waved goodbye, and I saw him scratch his head and say, "I could've sworn that squirrel just waved at me."

"You're crazier than the squirrel, man," Ben said.

"You know they don't understand you."

"I know, I know, but I miss him so much, Squeaky."

"I'm sorry, bud, we just have to deal with the cards we have."

"I know," I said.

We managed to gather quite a bit of corn to take back to the others at the hideout. We added it to the pile they started a long time ago.

"Let's go have a look at the palace from the outside, if it's not risky?" I asked Tonito.

"I'm pretty sure I can get y'all close enough to see it. We'll have to go across the tops of the buildings to get to it. Please keep one eye on the sky the whole time," he said.

The climb to the top of the building was not as bad as I expected. Now the jump from building, that was another story. We all knew my jumping abilities were lacking a little. I cleared the gap between the buildings with no problems. We came to the last building before the palace, and the gap was enormous.

Tonito and Squeaky got a running start and cleared it only by inches. I hesitated, and it cost me. I missed the building by a foot

47

and fell directly into a fruit stand below, knocking all the apples and oranges to the ground. The people around me were screaming, trying to kick me away. All I was doing was trying to get away! Finally, I made it down the alley behind the building I missed, but in all the commotion, I drew the attention of a big house cat standing outside of the palace. I was assuming a guard of some sort in the palace.

"He's here!" I heard him say, and three more cats came running my way. The only place I could go was in the hole of a barrel that was turned upside down.

"We've got him now! He can't go anywhere. He's trapped." They tried to tip the barrel over, but it was too heavy for them.

"Run, go get help," one cat said to another. "We'll stay here and make sure he doesn't escape."

I knew I had to do something before he came back with help. About that time, an arrow barely missed one of the cats stuck in the side of the barrel. *Squeaky*, I thought. The next arrow hit its mark and made one cat scream and run off down the alley. The other cat hid behind the barrel, so Squeaky couldn't see him to get a shot.

About that time, I heard a loud bark. Columbo! He ran into the barrel, knocking it over, then taking off after the cat that was hiding behind it.

"Let's go!" Squeaky shouted. "Here comes the others!"

I took off on the side of the building and followed Tonito and Squeaky to this hole in the side of the building. "That was close!" I said.

Tonito said, "We're not safe yet. They have flooded the streets with animals looking for you."

"What do we do?" Squeaky asked.

"Let me think," Tonito said.

"Tony, you think you could get Pesco to the water's edge?"

"Now?"

"Yes," I said. "All his animals are on the street, perfect time to sneak into the palace."

"Great idea, Pibby, but y'all are not gonna like how we have to go to get there," Tonito said.

"Doesn't matter. Let's go!"

PIBBY'S ADVENTURES

A few minutes later, I was taking my words back as we were crawling through the sewer pipes toward the stream. "I told you, you weren't gonna like it!" We walked while holding our noses, trying not to throw up. Finally, we were at the water's edge, and Tonito slapped the tree three times.

Pesco emerged and said, "I said tomorrow, Tony."

"I know, but we've got to go now! They're all out on the streets looking for us."

"Okay, but I'm gonna warn y'all. I haven't eaten my lunch yet. I'm not responsible for what may happen."

"We'll just have to chance it!" I said. "I hear them coming!"

"Okay, jump in!" Pesco opened his mouth, and we jumped in just in time before they surrounded Tonito.

We peeked out barely outta of the water.

"Where are they?" the biggest cat demanded.

"They swam across the stream and disappeared into that brush there," Tonito said, pointing.

"Go!" the cat said to all the others. "Search it good! You! You're going with me."

They took Tonito away, and we submerged heading to the palace. Pesco swam at a slow steady pace, trying not to cause any water disturbance.

"I sure hope this fish doesn't get hungry," I said as I drew my sword just in case.

Squeaky drew his arrow out of his quiver and said, "I won't go down easy, literally."

I chuckled as we sat there in the dark, waiting. Pesco's throat started pulsating, trying to pull us down farther in his mouth. I gave the roof of his mouth a good poke with my sword, and the pulsating stopped. I couldn't help to be worried about Tonito. I hope he could convince them he wasn't helping us, or worse, make him give up the plan.

I could tell we were getting close because Pesco slowed down. We could feel him starting to move up toward the bank. Pesco opened his mouth, and we jumped out on the bank and thanked Pesco.

49

He said, "Come back to this same place and hit the water three times, and I'll come."

"Okay, now go eat something please!"

CHAPTER 8

The Palace

The place was so dark you couldn't see where your next step should be. We could barely see light in the outline of a door, so we headed toward it. The door hadn't been opened in a long time, but it wasn't locked. We pushed the door open halfway, just far enough so we could get in. The only light we had was from the floor above us.

Making the least amount of noise, we eased up the stairs to the next floor. Squeaky turned the knob, and it wasn't locked either. Squeaky pushed the door open slowly, and we heard voices coming from the next room. These rooms were small. It looked like they made them that way after they occupied the closed building.

"The emperor wants everyone up top to look for these to scrawny squirrels," one of the animals said.

"Well, let's go then. A lot of trouble for two country squirrels. What they gonna do? Hit us with a cane pole?" they said while laughing. They left slamming the next door as they were leaving.

"Who are they calling scrawny?" Squeaky balked. "Don't they know I'm chubby?"

Laughing, I said, "Reckon not, now pick up your cane pole and come on!"

We covered the next few floors with no problems. Then we heard this nagging, complaining, whiny voice coming from a room way back at the end of the hall.

"I told you, if you don't let me out, my dad, the black guardian, will come here and kill every one of you! Now let me out this minute!" Solace shouted.

Squeaky said, "That's definitely her!"

I pushed open the door, and they had her tied up in a cage about twice her size. She was petite, very neat, with blue eyes. I never saw a squirrel with blue eyes. The blue dress she was wearing really matched her beautiful blue eyes.

"Pibby! Pibby! What are you daydreaming about?" Squeaky yelled. "Cut her loose and let's get out of here."

"Who are you?" she yelled. "Don't you dare touch me! Do you know who my father is! He'll have your head!"

"Calm down, Solace. Your father sent us to save you. Now quit yelling and come with us," I said, whispering.

"Us?"

"Squeaky and me."

"Squeaky? From the grove? There's no way my father would send him to save me. He's just a gatherer of foods for the grove," she sneered.

"If you don't shut up and follow us, I'll leave you right here!"

"You can't talk to me that way!"

"Bye!" I said, walking out the door.

"Wait! I'm coming."

We put her in between us as we made our way back down to the stream.

"Where are we going? I can't see anything! You don't have any idea where we're going, do you?" she said, complaining.

Reaching the door to the stream, we stepped out onto the muddy bank again.

"My dress is getting mud on it, and my shoes are full of water! What are we doing down here?" she asked.

"Catching a ride!" I said as I hit the water three times.

"On what?"

"A fish," I said. "We gonna ride in a big ole fish's mouth." I hit the water three times again, still no Pesco. "Hold on, I'll be back." I dove in the water and swam toward the water entrance. "What's this?" It was a gate. It had been let down so nothing could get through.

I swam back to the bank. "They know we're here. They've put down the gates to block the water entrance."

"What are we gonna do, Pibby?" Squeaky asked.

"Find another way out, I guess. We can't stay here any longer. Let's go!"

We pulled Solace through the mud back to the room we got her from. We started moving upward, floor after floor, no one.

Solace said, "This place has many floors before you get to the ground level."

We finally made it to the door to the top level.

"Get ready, Squeaky, we may need to fight our way out this time!"

"I'm ready. Stay behind, Solace."

"Where's the Squeaky I knew?" she questioned.

We slammed open the door, and two raccoons grabbed us and held us down, taking my sword and Squeaky's bow.

"Ah! Just in time for the wedding!" the emperor said. "Take her and get her ready to marry her mate."

"I never marry the likes of you!" Solace screamed as they took her to one of the side rooms.

I couldn't move as they both were on top of me, holding me down.

"Heroes! Ha! Just two squirrels from the country is all I see. Let them up, boys. They're not crazy enough to do anything now. I want you to witness this so you can go back and tell the guardian it was too late. You couldn't take her. That is the only way you'll leave here with your lives. Take it or leave it," the emperor demanded.

"Okay, we'll take it. She is anything but a gripe anyway!" Squeaky yelled.

I remained silent because I knew I would die trying to save her today.

"Good choice, good choice. Now eat and drink as you please. You will need it for your trip back."

"I want my bow back!"

"Your weapons will be waiting at the entrance when I allow you to leave," he said.

I walked toward the emperor. "And why marry her? There's thousands out there just like her."

"No, not like her. Her mom was part human, which makes her more capable of learning and teaching ways to improve our lives as animals. Therefore, she will make a perfect mother to my children," the emperor answered.

"How can you marry someone who doesn't want to marry you?"

"Stick around, I'll show you!" He laughed.

Squeaky walked over and said, "Forget it, Pibby. We're done. Let's just go home," pulling me to the side.

"Let's eat everyone!" the emperor demanded.

Squeaky pulled me to the side and said, "Look at the back of the crowd, Tonito and all the boys from the hideout."

We didn't dare walk over to them; it might give us away. I looked at Tonito. He had my sword stuck in his belt around his side. Squeaky's bow was draped over to the next animal's shoulder. I started eating, making my way to the other side of the room. Squeaky was stuffing his face, a few feet from me.

I got across the table from Tonito and whispered, "Wait till Solace is back out here, and I'll give you the sign when." Tonito nodded and moved back to other side of the room. "Get ready, Squeaky," I whispered.

"Everyone, can I get your attention? Would you please welcome Ms. Solace to the room."

Solace came out in this long blue dress that matched her blue eyes like before. She looked radiant, fit for a king.

"Pibby! You're daydreaming again! When are we gonna do this?" Squeaky asked.

"I'll move closer so I can grab Solace. You work toward the squirrel with your bow." I made my way beside Solace, grabbed her, and said, "Now!"

Solace and I ran toward Tonito, and he threw me my sword. I started making my way to the back of the room.

"Y'all get out. We'll try to hold them off!" Tonito yelled.

PIBBY'S ADVENTURES

Squeaky had already stuck two of the guard coons in the legs with arrows, making his way to us. "Let's go while we can!"

It was an all-out brawl in the room. The emperor was barking orders and standing behind a column.

We were about to leave the room when Squeaky said, "Hold on!" He took aim with his bow at the emperor. With a shot all the way across the room, he hit his mark, and the emperor went down without anyone noticing.

"Amazing," I said. "Let's go!"

We made our way out the front door, running as fast as we could. The guards outside noticed us and gave chase. There were way too many to fight. Just as we were about to turn and face them, we heard, "Over here, jump in!"

Pesco was at the bank with his mouth wide open, screaming, "Jump!" We ran and jumped as far as we could. Pesco closed his mouth and sank just as we landed. Breathing as hard as we could, we sat there while Pesco carried us out of the city.

After about an hour, we felt Pesco swimming up toward the bank. We jumped out on the bank somewhere just outside the city. Pesco said, "Hopefully, this will give you a good enough head start. I wish you all the best, princess."

"Thanks, Pesco, you saved our lives. We will forever be grateful," Solace said, blowing him a kiss.

"Thanks, bud, we'll see you again," I said.

"Go!" he said.

We all took to running toward the tree line, and once we made it there, we ran some more. All the while, my mind was on our friends from the hideout and the sacrifices they made. After running all day, we settled down in a large hole way back in a tree. Not a word was uttered. We just sat and stared at each other, hearts racing and eyes full of tears for our friends. Then off to sleep we went, without saying a word.

I woke up first, and going back over to what happened yesterday, I thought maybe when they saw what happened to the emperor, they all just quit and went their own ways. Wishful thinking probably, but just maybe, that's what happened.

Solace woke up next and thanked Squeaky, now waking up, and me for saving her. "I hope your friends are okay," she said. "They are very brave, as are you two."

"What do we do now?" Squeaky asked.

"I don't exactly know where we are, but we know we have to travel east. The truth is, we could be way out of line with the grove. East is a start in the right direction anyway. Let's find food, pack our sacks, and be on our way."

"I can't travel in this stupid wedding dress. I can hardly run, much less climb."

"I have some old jeans, and I have an old shirt Mr. Mudar gave me," I answered.

"That'll do," she said.

We left the hole so Solace could change into her new old clothes.

"Maybe the trip back will be easier," I said to Squeaky.

"I wouldn't count on it, bud," he said. "We have a little more baggage this time."

Looking back at the hole, I heard, "Squeaky! Don't worry about me. I can carry my weight, boys. Just try to keep up with me!" Solace popped out of the hole, looking like an angel with jeans on. I stared the whole time she was climbing down.

"You're doing it again! You've gotta focus, man!" Squeaky said, laughing.

"We better go. We have no idea what's on the other side of these woods. Keep your eyes peeled and your bow ready, Squeaky!"

The terrain was kinda bushy and around the height of our shoulders, but it was like that everywhere we looked. I took my sword and beat us a path out ahead. Solace didn't complain at all. I thought she was kinda humbled knowing how hard it was leaving our friends back there.

"How did you end up in town anyway, Solace?" Squeaky asked.

"Well, I was out looking for flowers and such for our hole home. I just kinda lost track of time and direction. I ended up near the hard road with all the machines on it. Suddenly, Roka showed up, swooping down, grabbing me barely by my shirt. He flew over the road with me, and my shirt was torn, and I fell right in the back of one the moving machines. I guess that saved my life, but I ended up in town when the machine stopped. I jumped out, but I was immediately taken by the emperor's cats. The emperor saw my eyes, and he knew I wasn't a normal squirrel."

"Cars!"

"What?" Solace asked.

"Those machines are called cars, trucks, or just vehicles. The roads are called highways."

"How do you know all this?" she asked.

"I'm not normal either. I was once a boy."

"What! You're like my mother was!"

"I think so, but I'm not sure how or if all this is real. I'm kinda just rolling with it," I said.

"Squeaky, did he hit his head during the escape?"

"Must have!" Squeaky laughed.

It was rough going and slow. We decided to find some food we took to the trees, trying to spot some sorta acorn or walnut tree. Not one could be found.

"I sure would like to be at Mr. Mudar's table right about now, with carrots, nuts, pecans, sweet potatoes, butter beans."

"Butter beans?" Solace yelled.

"The squirrel loves butter beans!" Squeaky said, laughing.

"You're a little weird, Pibby."

"Thanks, Ms. Solace," I said.

"Crab apples!" Squeaky shouted.

We all climbed down to the crab apple tree, grabbed one a piece, and started eating.

"Well, save some for us!" The family of deer came walking in slowly. It was a doe and two fawns.

"Sure," I said. "I'll knock off a few to the ground for your babies."

"Thanks, that's very thoughtful of you," the deer said. "Don't think I've ever seen any of you in these woods."

"We're just passing through on our way back home."

"Where do you call home?" she asked.

"The grove."

"Oh my! You're a long way from home, aren't you?"

"We aren't really sure exactly where we are, to tell you the truth," I said.

She said, "You're headed in the right direction, but there's a big gorge up ahead that you'll have to find a way to cross. If you go around, it'll take you weeks out of your way."

"Well, we better be going. I need to get these two bedded down for the day. Thanks for all your help," I said.

We ate till we didn't wanna see another crab apple and went on our way. Surely this gorge thing won't be that big. At least for our sakes, I hope it was not.

CHAPTER 9

This Is for the Birds

"My goodness! What a hole! That's the biggest hole I've ever seen!" Solace shouted. The gorge was at least a mile wide and deep. "We've got to go around, right?" she asked.

"What about through it? It won't take as long," I said. "Let's walk down the edge of it a ways and see if it gets any easier. Y'all go that way. I'll go this way."

We went searching for a better way to cross. I went by myself one way; they went the opposite. I walked for a while and came up on a spot that would be a little easier to get down this side of the gorge. I headed back to tell them. About that time, I heard a scream; it was Solace. I looked up and a hawk had swooped down and grabbed her from the side of the gorge. I ran over to Squeaky. He had his bow aimed at the hawk.

"Whoa! Let's see where he takes her." They dropped her at the bottom of the gorge. She quickly got up and ran for cover under the cliff side.

"Solace! Are you okay?" I shouted.

"Yes, but this hawk is coming back."

"Just take cover and stay there. We're coming!" It was gonna take us all day to get to her, and the hawk was still in the area, so we had to be aware of his location while climbing down.

Squeaky said, "I'll go down over here, you go there. Maybe you'll draw him to you and get a shot on him." Squeaky was showing

59

that there was more to him than meets the eye. This little guy was nothing you wanted to tangle with, especially with that bow in his hand.

"Good idea!" I said, heading down a ways from him.

We started down the gorge at the same time. The hawk was still stalking Solace. You could hear her scream when he swooped in close. Squeaky and I were going as fast as we could, but it was pretty dangerous, even for squirrels like us. One slip, and it was straight down. Suddenly, a hawk swooped down over my head from the rear.

"Another hawk, Squeaky!"

"I've got one over my head too!" Squeaky shouted.

They had us all three pinned down. Then I saw the one over Squeaky go down in a spiraling motion. Squeaky had hit his mark with the arrow.

"Draw him in!" Squeaky yelled.

I stood up so the hawk could see me clearly. The hawk was coming full speed directly at me. I didn't budge. Squeaky's arrow went in one eye and out the other. The hawk fell just in front of me. "Wow! What a shot!" I yelled.

"Let's go get Solace now," he said.

In what seemed like hours, we made it to the bottom of the gorge. The hawk had perched himself just above where Solace was hiding.

"Good try, little ones, but we can wait all day," the hawk said as two more landed beside him.

We took off toward Solace and hid in her little hole with her.

"You can't hide forever. I'll tell you what, just sacrifice one of your friends. We'll let the other two go," the hawk said.

About that time, Squeaky shot out the hole, turned around, and drove an arrow through a hawk's head. "I can do this all day!" Squeaky yelled.

"Hope you have a lot of arrows!" the hawk said as five more hawks landed beside him.

"What are we gonna do, Pibby? I don't see a way out!"

"I don't know, Squeaky."

Solace was crying in the back. "I don't wanna die."

PIBBY'S ADVENTURES

"Just send out one. That's all." The hawk laughed.

Time went by pretty fast, and more and more hawks were gathering at the gorge. Apparently, we happened upon a roost where they all slept. Suddenly, I felt a vibration in the ground below me, and a mole stuck his head from the ground.

"Well, hello, my good fellows and lady. Looks like you got yourselves in a bit of a pickle. I'm here to help you out of it!" he said. "My name is Ticker, and you must be the heroes and the lost princess of the grove."

"You know us?" Solace asked.

"Everyone knows about how love drove him to risk his life to save his one true love."

"One true love? I've never seen him in my life before this! One true love! Huh?" Solace asked, looking at me.

I just shrugged my shoulders and shook my head.

"Aw, look, their first lovers' quarrel," Squeaky said, laughing.

"Shut up!" I said.

"Okay, okay! We've got to get a move on. It's gonna be pretty tight, but you should be able to get through the tunnel I've dug. Follow me."

"Squeaky, you go first to widen out the tunnel a little," I said, laughing.

"Picking on the chubby squirrel!" he said.

We followed Ticker to an open room under the ground to rest.

"We're about halfway out. Let's stay here tonight. The hawks will lose interest and spread out to hunt in the morning. It'll be a lot safer to travel aboveground then. I don't have any food that you probably eat unless you have the appetite for an earthworm?"

"We'll just wait till tomorrow," Solace said with a face.

"I'm going to my family now. When you start back, just follow the tunnel. It'll lead you to the surface," Tinker said.

"We can't thank you enough. You saved our butts today."

"Anything for the lovers and the archer," he said, disappearing in the tunnel.

"Oh my gosh! How did this rumor get started?"

Squeaky said, "Pibby saw your picture and has been in love ever since! You're all he talks about! 'Oh, she's so beautiful, and those eyes, I could stare at her all day!'"

"You done, Squeaky?" I said, staring at him. "Animals talk, and sooner or later, the story gets twisted. I guess they just figured that someone wouldn't risk their life for someone they didn't love."

"So why do you risk your life for me?"

"To be able to stay in the grove, the guardians said it was the only way I could stay."

Solace acted like that answer hurt her feelings and didn't say a thing for the rest of the night.

I looked at Squeaky and said, "What did I say?" He shrugged his shoulders and went to sleep. I closed my eyes and eased off to sleep.

CHAPTER 10

The Boat (*The Ketri*)

The next morning, I woke up early and ventured out to see what was going on aboveground. Squeaky and Solace were still asleep in the mole room underground. When I poked my head aboveground, I heard nothing at all. It was as quiet as could be, no movement at all. We were on the other side of the gorge, just like Ticker had said. It was as flat as it could be as far as I could see. I knew food and water was gonna be a factor soon, so I started looking for something to at least tide us over.

Squeaky woke up next and came out and called out my name. "Over here!" I shouted.

Squeaky came over to where I was and asked, "What are you doing?"

"Just looking for breakfast," I said.

Solace joined us a little while later, and we were back on track to home. No trace of food or water could be found. The terrain was dry and hot. We had to find at least water pretty soon. We crossed several pastures till we came up on this old abandoned farm. No one had been here in a long time. Everything was falling in and rotting down.

"I'll look around for some old fruit trees or well at least. There's gotta be something to drink or eat around here."

Solace shouted, "Look! An old pool. It's got some water in the bottom of it."

Before I could say anything, she had run over and started drinking out of it. "What if it's contaminated?"

"What does that mean?" she asked.

I said, "Water can go bad and really make you sick or worse. See how green it is, smells bad also."

"I feel fine, Pibby! There's nothing wrong with the water!"

"Yeah, it's fine!" Squeaky said, drinking from the pool.

"Well, I'm not drinking it!"

"Suit yourself!" they said, laughing.

There was no food to be found, so we got back on the trail. We finally came to a tree line where we found wild berries and nuts. The rain started about the time we reached the hole we intended to stay in tonight. Squeaky and Solace started feeling bad soon after we settled in. Keeping the food down they just ate wasn't an option.

"What do we do?" Squeaky yelled. "I'd go outside and find fresh water."

"It's raining! There's your water," I said. I settled in while they stayed sick all night long.

The next morning started with the sunshine returning and me pigging out on some blueberries and acorns. The other two didn't have an appetite for some reason. They reluctantly followed while I made my way through the woods.

Knowing they weren't really up to traveling today, I said, "Let's just relax today. I think I hear a stream up ahead. We'll stop and let you two recuperate."

We found the stream and sat beside it, rehashing on how I warned them about the water and how they were tired of hearing me reminding them of it. Watching the stream went by, I got an idea. "This is the same stream that goes near the grove, right?"

"I think so," Squeaky said.

"So why don't we take it?"

"I don't swim very well," Solace mourned.

"No! Build something to float down it! Like when we escaped Shonta's snake hole. This stream could take us miles away, but it's got to end up near the grove, right?" I questioned the two.

PIBBY'S ADVENTURES

Squeaky said, "I guess so, but who knows what we'll go through getting there?"

"Well, I vote on we build a float, take that chance. What do you say, you two?"

"If it means not walking anymore, I'm in!" Solace said.

"Okay! I'm with the crowd. Let's look for something big enough that we can all fit on comfortably."

"Y'all look, I'm resting!" Solace sighed.

Squeaky and I began searching the area for things to build a float. I came across this flat board about two feet across and same length.

Squeaky said, "Need something to attach to it to stay out of the rain and sun during the day."

We took sticks and made a sort of lean-to on the back of the board. We padded it with moss and leaves for comfort. I fashioned a rudder out of a limb so we could guide it down the stream. Then we had two long limbs to help with the steering.

"Let's gather some food to store under the lean-to so we won't have to stop so often," I said, looking at Solace.

"Okay, okay!" she said.

When we finished, we had a pretty secure-looking float boat. I had my worries about our decision, but we didn't really know where we were right now, so what the heck?

"We have to name it," I said.

"Name it?" Solace asked.

"Bad luck not to name it. How 'bout you, Squeaky? What do you wanna call it?"

"How 'bout *The Ketri*? After my mom," he said, lowering his head.

How could we disagree with that? So we all agreed to call it *The Ketri*. "All aboard *The Ketri*!" I shouted.

We all climbed aboard. Squeaky and I pushed it from the bank, and we were off in the current of the stream, headed to heaven knows where. Most of the first day was smooth sailing, easygoing, calm, and quiet. Little did we know what was around the bend. We came around the corner, and there was a bridge with a long dark tunnel

65

going under it. It didn't have much clearance, so we had to steer our boat really precise. We cleared the sides and made it in the tunnel.

The tunnel was total darkness. Solace hid in the lean-to. Squeaky and I got as low as we could. We were bouncing off the sides and scraping the top of the tunnel. There was a light way down at the end of the tunnel, but there was something else also. Eyes! A pair of yellow eyes about halfway to the exit of the tunnel.

"Well, what do we have here? Floating dinner? This is the first time I've had dinner delivered," the gator said. He opened his mouth wide, waiting for us to float right in.

Squeaky shouted, "I can't see to shoot my bow!"

I pulled my sword out just in time to drive it through the roof of his mouth when he clamped down on us. He quickly opened his mouth. I pulled the sword out and stuck him again. The gator backed off and dove under us. The raft cleared the tunnel, and the gator surfaced right behind us. He swam our way to attack again. Squeaky drove an arrow deep into one his eyes, and he quickly dove again. I got on the rudder to steer us, all the time looking for the gator to return. Squeaky stood with his bow drawn, waiting.

Solace, still hiding, asked, "Is he gone?"

"I think so," Squeaky said, still scanning the water.

The raft picked up speed in the current, and we all breathed a big sigh of relief. I didn't think about gators and such before I made the suggestion of the raft. About that time, two ducks swam up, one on either side of us.

"That's was a close call, friends!" they said. "We saw it all as we were landing back there."

"Are their many gators in this stream?" Solace asked.

"They mainly hang out near the bridges. It's easy for them to get out and sun around them. You should be okay for a while. There's no another bridge for ten miles or so," the duck said.

Squeaky asked, "Have you ever heard of the grove?"

They both shook their heads no. "Is that where you're headed?"

"Yes, we really have no idea where or how far it is from here."

"We don't usually stray too far from our roost, so we really can't say what's downstream. There is a dangerous stretch ahead though.

PIBBY'S ADVENTURES

The stream runs through a wide open field, and Sova patrols it regularly."

"Sova! He's alive! No way!" Squeaky said. I just acted surprised.

"Well, we haven't seen him for about six or seven days, but he does patrol it usually," they said.

"How many days has it been, Pibby?" Squeaky asked.

"I'm not sure, Squeaky."

"Well, I hope he's alive so I can drive an arrow through his head!"

"We'll let y'all be on your way. Be careful, hope you make it home!" they said, swimming away.

I needed to tell Squeaky about the deal I made with Sova, but hopefully, it wouldn't come to that.

"Let's pull over and build our lean-to a little bigger to hide us from anything in the air. Maybe put limbs all over it to make it blend in a little more," I said.

"It doesn't matter. I'm gonna shoot him the minute I see him!" Squeaky said.

"We'll do it, just in case."

"Good idea!" Solace said.

The Ketri looked totally different when we finished. It looked like a floating bush to me. After eating and talking about how close we came to being dinner for the gator, we pushed off. We have gotten to where we feel immune to danger, seemed like it was around every corner. I personally was hoping this one would be different.

As we rounded the corner to the open field, we all ducked inside our lean-to. Squeaky kept a sharp look on the sky, hoping to see Sova. Solace and I were thinking the opposite. We traveled the whole length of the field, no Sova.

"He's probably too scared!" Squeaky shouted.

The stream entered a thick head of woods after the field. It was getting dark, so we tied *The Ketri* off to a tree branch and lay on the moss we brought with us. It had been a crazy first day on the stream. *Wonder what tomorrow will bring?* I thought as I drifted off to sleep. Squeaky just lay there, staring at the top of the lean-to, still mad that Sova didn't show.

The next morning, we woke up, and Squeaky wasn't on the raft. I jumped up, ran outside the lean-to, and called his name. When he didn't answer, I followed his tracks to a tree right before the open field. I found him at the top of the tree, looking for Sova.

"He's just too scared to come out!" Squeaky shouted.

"Squeaky, I need to tell you something. I made a deal with Sova when I went back. I would fix his wing if he would tell me where Mr. Lapin was and would let us back through when we come back. It was the only way I could save Mr. Lapin."

"You made that deal, I didn't. I'm glad you saved him so I can take him out."

"I guess you're right, but don't let your anger get in the way of your judgment, buddy. You ready to go?" I said.

"Okay, let's go," he said, frustrated.

I was glad I got that off my shoulders, but he was right; he didn't make that deal. *The Ketri* was off and running again. It was real thick and great place for an ambush, so Solace stayed inside, and we kept our eyes open. The stream got real shallow for a few times, so Squeaky and I would jump off and pull *The Ketri* along. The princess stayed inside. We didn't know it, but the stream was swinging way around and miles from our path home. It felt safe, so we stayed the course.

The next few days were pretty uneventful. We'd travel during the day and tie up and sleep at night. When we needed food, we'd stop and gather enough for a couple days. We came around a bend in the stream, and we could see a farm up above us.

"Let's tie up and go look to see if we can pass through safely," I said, talking to Squeaky.

Solace said, "I know, I know, stay in the boat."

Squeaky and I slipped up on the side of the stream to the farm. We came to an old barn but no farmhouse or sign of anyone.

"It's looks fine, Pibby. Let's go get the boat."

"Okay," I said.

It was about that time when we heard talking around the other side of the barn. We climbed the back side of the barn and up to

PIBBY'S ADVENTURES

the top to see where the voices were coming from. It was about ten squirrels in a circle, just jabbering about anything.

"I bet I can spit farther than you," one said.

"Well, I bet I can jump from that tree to that one," said another.

One squirrel with a long thin spear said, "I'll split that pear while it sits on your head."

"No way!" said another.

The brave soul put the pear on his head and backed up against a tree. "Try it!" he shouted.

About that time, Squeaky's arrow split the pear from the top of the barn.

"Wow! Who did that?" they all shouted.

Squeaky was already on the ground walking toward them. "Squeaky's the name," he said proudly. This is my friend, Pibby."

I said, "Hi, nice to meet y'all."

"Where did you learn to shoot that thing like that?"

"An old rabbit taught me a while back."

"Never seen you around here, where are you from?"

"Just upstream a ways." Not wanting to hear the heroes' praise, Squeaky left it at that.

"We're the Acorn Hill family. We're all family in some way or another. This place is called Acorn Hill. Guess you can see why they call it that. There were oak trees far as you could see. Most of the older ones stay close to the top of the hill. We hang out round this old barn. What are you doing 'round these parts?"

"We kinda got lost and tried to take the stream back home."

"Well, that thing winds a thousand times around these hills. Gonna take you a while that way," he said. "If you're going west, it's best to cut through the hills right there. It goes right by Mr. Lapin's place in about two days."

"You say Mr. Lapin?" Squeaky and I said at the same time.

"He was the one who taught me to shoot this thing. Have you seen him lately?" Squeaky asked.

"No, haven't seen him in a few weeks. Course we don't go that far from the hill often," he said.

69

About that time, they all got quiet and stared at something behind us. Solace had been listening from the barn.

"This mean that we're walking again!" She sighed.

None of the Acorn Hill family said a word.

"I guess so. It's a lot closer to home," I said.

"Look at her eyes. They are blue as can be! It must be her! The princess! This must be Pibby! And Squeaky! Y'all are legends! The stories of all the close calls and how you saved the love of your life!" they all shouted.

"Here we go!" Squeaky said.

"Yes! He rescued me from certain death! Our love can't be denied! And Squeaky, the brave warrior! He shot the emperor from two miles away!" Solace had them in a trance. She grabbed me and hugged me tight, then kissed me, and said, "My heroes!"

I whispered, "What are you doing?"

"I'm making us legends!" She laughed.

I couldn't deny, the hug and the kiss were not the worst thing that had ever happened to me.

"Tell us more!" they shouted.

I bet she talked for an hour about how close we came to death and the great escapes we had made. The Acorn Hill family was clinging to her every word.

"Y'all have got to stay the night. You can stay right there in the barn. We'll gather some food and have celebration! Will you stay?" they shouted.

I looked at Squeaky and Solace; they were smiling from ear to ear. "I guess so!" I shouted back.

Everyone shouted, "Hooray!"

CHAPTER 11

The Legends

They prepared for the next two hours. They brought fruits, nuts, and vegetables. We had fresh milk, cold water, and a soft place to sit around a fire.

Squeaky got into the storytelling and may have stretched it a little bit. Everyone was laughing, joking, and eating. Then the music started. Four of the brothers had made instruments and learned to play some. They all pointed to me and Solace to dance.

She grabbed my hand and said, "Why not? Let's make this legend grow!"

We all danced and sang and told stories into the night. Our legend was ten times what it was when we arrived. It all started settling down and someone asked, "How will you ever get back to Roka? Word is he has a whole pack waiting on you to return. Shonta's friends vow to be waiting on your return also. You know Sova wants revenge for what you did to him. How will you survive all that and get home?"

Everyone was very quiet and looked at us intently. I didn't know what to say because I didn't know how we could face that and survive. The mood around the fire changed that fast. Everyone was staring at the ground, thinking the worst.

"I don't know exactly how we'll make it home, but we will. Look at the friends we've made along the way. We can't let all of you and them down," I said.

"I'll shoot 'em all in the eyes!" Squeaky yelled.

Everyone shouted, "Shoot 'em all in the eyes!"

The singing and dancing started back and lasted for hours. The question was lingering in all three of our minds, *How on earth are we gonna make it home?* Odds were definitely against us making it through that a second time.

All of a sudden, I didn't feel like such a legend anyone. My friends meant the world to me now. I couldn't let them down. The party ended, and everyone went their own ways to their homes. We went inside the barn, crawled up to the loft, and found a soft spot in the hay to lie down. None of us went straight to sleep. We didn't say anything either, just lay there, wishing we were already home, already in the grove and safe. But no worries! We're the legends!

CHAPTER 12

Lapin's Lair

The morning came in what seemed like minutes. When we came out the barn, they had our boat sitting outside the barn.

"We'll keep it safe for you till you return. There's food and bedding in these sacks for your trip home." The whole family was there to see us off.

"Thank you for everything," I said. "We will see you again, I promise!" Solace and Squeaky said their goodbyes, and we grabbed our stuff. They pointed us in the right direction, and once again, we were headed home.

It was a sad moment in our journey because we had joined their family that night. I didn't know what the days ahead were gonna bring, but we were all thinking about it. The hills were steep, and the grass thick, but we were making a good time. I could see miles ahead of us, valleys and hills as far as I could see.

Solace kept looking back at me and smiling. That kiss was still running through my mind. I'd never cared for someone like her, but I'd die protecting her now. Squeaky and Solace were my family now, and nothing would get by me to harm them. I did miss my family on the farm, but I rarely thought about that life anymore. I wondered where they think I was. Did I die? I was sure it was not a dream now. I'd got to get them back to the grove first, then I'd figure all this out.

Squeaky held his hand up. "Stop! I saw movement up ahead." Squeaky went over to the nearest tree to get a better look. "It's cows, just cows!" he shouted.

We walked down to where the cows were grazing. "Just traveling through!" Squeaky said.

"Very well, come on through," they said.

I knew we were safe for a while. Cows could sense danger long before it shows. The cows meant we were on farmland, and the farm couldn't be too far from us. We finally saw the farm up ahead and decided to hit the trees to get closer. The family of the farm were outside having some sort of celebration. We sat in the tree above them, watching them sing happy birthday to an older man sitting at the end of table. It instantly made me think of my home.

Squeaky somehow knew my thoughts and said, "We better get going."

Then a loud *bang* rang out. *Bang!* The limbs above us exploded. *Bang!* The limbs below us exploded.

"They're shooting at us, get in that hole!" I said.

"Miss them!" the two boys shouted.

They went in the hole! *Bang!* They shot at the hole.

"Just stay back!" I said. "They'll leave when they get bored."

Bang! We listened as they went around shooting. Solace was in the back, shaking. I went back and hugged her and said, "It's okay, we're safe."

She started crying and said, "Why would they do that? We didn't do anything to them."

"It's what they do for food and sport."

"I want to leave!" She cried.

"Let's wait for a while, then we'll be on our way."

An hour passed, and we made our way out. There was no sign of the boys or anyone when we came out. We quickly made our way across the farm and back to the trail home. The grass fields turned to thick forest as we moved forward. Solace hadn't said a word since we left the farm. The forest was thick and dark; it looked familiar— Sova's forest.

"We're in Sova's forest!" I said out loud.

Squeaky looked around and said, "Are you sure?"

"Find a hole! Quick!" I said.

We hit the first hole we saw and listened for any sound of Sova. Nothing.

"Let's stay here tonight," I said.

"Maybe he'll show tomorrow!" Squeaky said, looking out the hole.

Solace lay down and dozed off to sleep. Squeaky and I just listened for Sova. I wondered if he would honor our deal or was he even alive. Either way, we would know tomorrow. Squeaky never slept and was ready to go first thing. There was no sign of Sova, so we climbed down and started toward Mr. Lapin's lair.

The way through this forest was a long one, and we knew it would take at least a day. Squeaky kept looking toward the sky, hoping.

Solace grabbed my hand and asked me, "What will you do when we make it home? Will you stay? Will you try to return to your farm someway?"

"I don't think the farm is an option anymore. Besides, I have a new reason to stay in the grove now."

"Oh yeah? What might that be?" Solace asked.

"I've met someone. You should see her beautiful blues," I said.

"Oh my goodness! Please be quiet!" Squeaky shouted. We all started laughing.

"Such a happy little family! I think I'll start crying!" It was Sova! We looked everywhere for him. We could hear him but not see him. "I've missed you two so much! Who's the pretty little blue-eyed one?"

"Come out, coward!" Squeaky shouted.

"Now that would be foolish of me, being you have your bow pulled. We had a deal, Pibby, didn't we?"

"Will you stand by it?" I shouted.

"Yes! You have no reason to doubt me," Sova said. "You have safe passage through my forest as promised."

Squeaky shouted, "I made no such deal with you!"

"Seems someone is holding a grudge for something I can't take credit for. I didn't kill your mother. I swooped down to get her, and she just vanished," Sova said.

"Sure, you expect me to believe a killer like you?" Squeaky shouted back.

"This bores me. You have safe passage, leave now!" Sova took flight from behind a large tree and disappeared in the sky.

"You trust him, Pibby?" Solace asked.

"We don't have any choice, we gotta go."

We had a long way to go to reach the forest's edge. I didn't know if Sova was true to his word, but we were gonna have to trust him. Squeaky led, Solace stayed in the middle, and I followed. We kept the pace up so we could get this over with. My sword was drawn; Squeaky's bow was out.

Every once in a while, we'd see a shadow fly over us. It was like he was making sure we were headed out. In my mind, I was thinking, I maybe should've finished the job when I had the chance. Mr. Lapin wouldn't be here if I had.

We reached the edge of the forest after walking all day. The next mile was all open pasture.

"Should we stay here till morning or try to make it across tonight?" I asked.

Squeaky said, "Let's try to make it tonight. It's not that far."

The sun was almost gone, and darkness was coming fast. We left the forest and started across the field, feeling our way through the darkness. Solace grabbed my hand and stayed closed to me. Suddenly, something hit my shoulder and knocked Solace and me to the ground. It grabbed Squeaky's shirt and flew away with him.

"Stay down!" I told Solace.

We crawled forward, slowly trying to find something to hide under. I yelled for Squeaky. No response.

"We had a deal! We had a deal!" I shouted. It had to be Sova going back on our deal. I finally stood up and pulled Solace to her feet. "Let's find somewhere to hide tonight." No sooner than when I said it, we got hit again. They missed again.

Solace started running, and I took off behind her. We could her it swooping down and barely missing us.

"In here! In here!" We heard a voice calling. It was Mr. Lapin standing at the entrance of a hole in the ground. "In here!" We ran down the hole behind Mr. Lapin till we reached a small lighted room.

"Squeaky?" he asked.

I shook my head no. "I think Sova grabbed him."

Mr. Lapin said, "We can't look tonight. There are beddings over by the wall. You two get some rest. I know it's been a hard night."

"Squeaky! Poor Squeaky!" Solace said, crying.

We don't know he had him by the shirt. We'll find him tomorrow, I kept telling myself that in my mind, but I knew the odds were against him. Sova was a deadly predator. Squeaky was pretty tough himself; he wouldn't go down easy.

Solace had gone to sleep with her head on my shoulder. Mr. Lapin was lying on a pile of grass in the corner. Sleeping wasn't on my mind, saving Squeaky was. I hoped he was okay. Morning couldn't have come soon enough for me.

Soon as daylight showed itself, I was on the hunt for Squeaky. Mr. Lapin went one way, Solace and I another. We covered the whole field to the edge of the forest. Nothing anywhere. We met Mr. Lapin back at his hideout hole. He motioned me to the side while Solace went down the hole to rest.

"I found this. It was Squeaky's bow. I didn't want her to see it. No sense of upsetting her," Lapin said.

"Where did you find it?"

"In the edge of the forest, a little ways in."

"Sova! He has to have him! Maybe there's still time. I've got to go in the forest. Can Solace stay here with you?"

"You know she can," he said. "You sure you wanna do this, Pibby?"

"I've got to! Tell Solace I'll be back as soon as I find Squeaky."

"Watch your back, and here, take his bow with you," Lapin said.

I turned and left running, no time to waste. I figured I'd go back to the place he had put Mr. Lapin when he had taken him. Maybe I could deal with Sova again if it wasn't too late. *Hang on, Squeaky, hang on.* I ran as fast as my legs would carry me After a while, I came to the edge of the forest. It was dark and thick, like I remembered. I didn't hesitate a bit. If Squeaky was alive, I was gonna find him.

CHAPTER 13

Squeaky's Fate

I was as quiet as I could be as I made my way through the forest. I knew I had to get there fast and quiet at the same time. Sova may toy with him a little but not long before he—well, I didn't wanna think about it.

The place I was looking for was just ahead, so I slowed down and crawled up to the tree next to the one I found Mr. Lapin in. Squeaky was nowhere in sight. I searched all the surrounding trees, no Squeaky.

"Sova! Sova!" I yelled as loud as I could. "Nothing. What should I do? Should I go back and give up? Keep searching the forest? I don't know!" I said out loud.

"May I help you, little one?" Sova's voice rang through the trees.

"Let Squeaky go! You made a deal with me!" I screamed.

"Whatever are you talking about? I haven't even seen your little friend."

"You're lying! Where is he? You grabbed him last night in the field right outside the forest."

"Sorry to say that wasn't me although I did see a lot of hawks in the area yesterday."

"Hawks?" I asked.

"They usually stay out of this area, being it's my hunting grounds. There were five or six around here yesterday."

PIBBY'S ADVENTURES

"Oh no! The hawks from the gorge, we escaped them a few days ago. Squeaky took care of a few of them at the quarry," I said.

"Hawks are a very tight-knit family. If you harmed one, you harmed them all. They aren't likely to give up till they get their revenge," Sova replied.

"I must get to the gorge! I don't remember how to get there though."

"Go west, which is that way, little one. It'll take you most of the day, I'm afraid. My advice is to go home. It's likely too late."

"I'll never give up! You take me. You could get me there fast," I said without thinking.

"Me? Take you to the gorge? Why on earth would I do that?" Sova laughed.

"Without me, you wouldn't be here. Some fox or coyote would've eaten you by now!"

"Good point, but I let you through the forest earlier. That was our deal. I held up my part of it."

"Sova, I need your help! Haven't you ever had a friend like Squeaky is to me? Come on! Just this one time!" I was kind of worried about exposing myself to Sova, but I had to trust him.

"Okay! Just this one time. I'll only take you there, then I'm gone. Now where are you? Let's get this over with."

I stepped out from behind the tree and stood there, not knowing if he was gonna eat me or help me.

"Turn around, I'll swoop down and grabbed your shirt, and we'll be off," Sova said.

I turned and closed my eyes and said, "Well, here goes nothing."

Sova swooped down and grabbed me with precise aiming. We were in the sky over the trees in no time. "Whoa!" I shouted. "This is awesome. You get to do this all your life? Why couldn't I have changed into a bird instead?"

"What are you talking about?"

"Nothing, this is great!" I said.

Sova flew twice as fast as I could run. We made it to the edge of the gorge, and he set me down behind a big rock. "Good luck, little one. I don't need to be seen in their feeding ground. There's too many of them to fight," Sova said, flying off.

Now I had to find Squeaky without letting them know I was here. Ticker! The mole! Maybe he could sneak me back in the gorge. I made my way around all the rocks to where we came out of Ticker's tunnel. There was no sign of Ticker, but the tunnel was still there. It was dark and very tight. I eased through it slow so it wouldn't cave in on top of me.

When I reached the end of the tunnel, I peeked out to see if any hawks were around. No signs of any of them, so I walked on out into the bottom of the gorge. "Squeaky!" I yelled. I figured I'd get some kinda reaction but nothing but my echo ringing back to me. Where could he be? Did they take him? What should I do now?

I decided to wait for the hawks to show up at sunset to roost here. Then I would get answers or get eaten. I found a place where nothing could see me and waited. The day was quickly going by and still no hawks. Finally, one of the hawks showed up and landed on the rim of the gorge. Then one by one, they covered the gorge walls. I didn't know how to do this without dying. I just shouted out, "I am looking for my friend Squeaky! Could you tell me where he is?"

"Well, I told y'all he would show up eventually," the hawk said. "All you have to do is grab something he loves. You take one, and you'll end up with both. Come out and let us see you!"

"No! Let Squeaky go!" I shouted. I knew it wasn't gonna be that easy, but I didn't know what to do. Fighting would be useless; pleading was the only thing I had.

The hawk motioned to another and flew somewhere and came back with Squeaky in his claws. He dropped him in the middle of the gorge and flew back up to the rim. Squeaky looked up at the hawk and laid his head back down.

I came out and went over to him. "Squeaky, you okay?" I asked.

He winked at me and said, "But don't let them know that."

"What have you done to him? He can hardly move!" I said. Hopefully, they'd believe he was hurt badly.

The hawks all flew down and circled us on the floor of the gorge. "Now it's time to exact some payback for our friends who are no longer here."

PIBBY'S ADVENTURES

I tossed Squeaky his bow, and I pulled my sword. "What are you waiting for!" I shouted.

"Brave little souls, aren't they?" The hawk laughed. "Okay, it's getting late, and our dinner is right in front of us. Let's eat!"

Suddenly, something swooped in and grabbed Squeaky and me by the collars and flew us out of the gorge. It was Sova! "Hold on, little ones, we may all die shortly."

The hawks were flying all around us, swooping in and reaching for us. Sova was faster, but there were too many of them. Sova was getting hit by their claws from both sides. Squeaky was taking one or two out with his bow and me with my sword.

"I've got to land somewhere!" Sova shouted.

"The barn! It was the barn we spent the night in. Down there!"

Sova swooped in the front door, and all our friends were waiting to close the two big front doors. The hawks were landing in the trees all around the barn. Sova fell over in the hay that was stored in the barn.

"He's hurt. Anyone know how to help him?"

"I'll see what I can do," someone said.

Squeaky said, "Don't help him!"

I looked at Squeaky and said, "He just saved your life, not now!"

"What do we do now? They have us surrounded!" Squeaky asked.

"We are safe right now. Everyone, calm down. Maybe they'll leave after a while." I hoped.

"We will wait and eat you one by one as you come out!" the hawk shouted.

Sova looked better after he rested for a bit. "Thanks," I told him as he stood up.

"I never had friends like you said before, so I thought I'd try to make a few," Sova said.

"Well, you have one now."

Someone built a fire, and we all sat around it to figure out what to do next. It reminded me of the great time we had a couple days ago. Solace came to my mind. I missed her dearly.

"Fire!" Squeaky said. "We can make torches and fight them off."

81

"We'll fight them off. You two, take the boat and hit the stream in the back. We fight them long enough for y'all to get down the stream a ways. We got plenty of food and water in here to stay for a while. They'll never know you left," Pibby said.

"What about Sova?" I asked.

"I'll get my strength back and leave. They can't catch me at full strength."

We all started making torches, enough for everyone to have two. Squeaky, two others, and I grabbed the boat and stood by the back door. They flung open the front doors, and all of them ran out the door with them. We took off toward the stream with the boat.

The hawks tried their best, but the fire kept them at bay. With the boat in the stream, Squeaky and I pushed off and quietly headed downstream.

They fought the hawks back for a good while and backed into the barn again and closed the doors. Squeaky and I were once again headed downstream on *The Ketri*. The others stayed in the barn for a few days, and the hawks left. Sova flew back to his forest a day later.

The stream winded back and forth through forests, fields, and hills. We didn't know if we should get off the boat and try to travel by land or stay on and see where it takes us. It seemed like the safer thing to do was to stay on the boat, so that was what we did.

Two days went by, and it seemed like we were going in circles because everything looked the same around us. We decided we were gonna get off at the next forest we went through. The next forest came a day later. We tied *The Ketri* off to a tree, gathered our things, and jumped off. There was a big fence around this forest, but it was easy for us to slip through it.

As we were walking, we noticed this forest was well taken care of. It was almost like it was someone's yard or something. After walking most of the day, we stopped like usual to find a hole to stay in for the night. After finding a hole, we settled in for the night. When the dark settled in, we noticed lights all over the forest and campfires everywhere.

What have we stumbled into? This can't be the city. It's behind us. Maybe it's a campground, I thought to myself. I didn't want to explain to Squeaky what a *campground* was. "We'll check it out in the morning. I'm pooped!" I told Squeaky. "Let's go to sleep."

"I'm with ya!" Squeaky sighed.

CHAPTER 14

The Campground

The next morning, we stayed in the trees and got closer to where the lights were coming from last night. It was a campground of some sorts. It looked like the Boy Scouts or something like it. There were several groups of boys broken up into small groups. We planned to just ease on through the forest above them. Suddenly, a rock hit me so hard that it knocked me out of the tree onto the ground below.

I didn't remember falling, but when I came to, I was in a small cage sitting on a picnic table. This young boy was telling his friend how he was gonna take me back home with him. I looked up to see if Squeaky was around anywhere. No Squeaky.

The boys came over poking sticks at me and shaking the cage. I was hoping they'd stick their finger in the cage so I could take a hunk out of it. They picked and prodded for a little while, then went off doing something else. All but one of them left. He was sitting all by himself by a tree. He wasn't talking to anyone or in any of the groups.

"I'll let you go, little fellow," he said, coming my way. "You don't belong in a cage. You belong in the trees."

Just as soon as he went to open my cage, a kid pushed him to the ground and said, "Leave my squirrel alone!"

"I was gonna let him go back to his family. That's all I was doing," the little one said.

"No!" the boy said. "I'm taking him home with me."

PIBBY'S ADVENTURES

I couldn't help feeling sorry for the little boy. I remembered getting picked on when I was a little boy. It was not very fun to be the one being picked on. You feel like you're the only one in the world.

The little boy got up and went to sit back down by the tree. I didn't quite understand how they saw and heard us one way. And we saw and heard ourselves another. At this time, I wished I was a boy so I could be this little boy's friend. Everyone deserves a friend.

Speaking of friends, where in the world was Squeaky? I sat there in that cage in the hot sun all day. The heat was starting to take effect on me 'cause I felt myself getting weak. The little boy had fallen asleep by the tree. Suddenly, I noticed a moment on the ground not far from the little boy. It was a big snake, likely from Shonta's crew.

"Don't bother that boy!" I shouted.

"My, my! Look who it is. Oh, I'll leave the boy alone, but I'll eat you." The snake headed my way and crawled up the table to the edge of the cage. "Can't run this time!"

Whack! The little boy hit the snake with a limb and nearly tore his head off. The snake fell to the ground and started toward the little boy. "No!" I said. Then an arrow split the snake's head into two. Squeaky! I looked up, and Squeaky was drawn back to shoot again if he had to. About that time, all the other boys came running up to see the snake.

They all were surprised that this little boy could kill a snake. "Tell us how you did it! Did it come after you? How did you know what to do?" They all gathered around him, asking questions. The little boy had a smile that covered his whole face.

"Come on! Let's go tell everyone how you killed the giant snake!" They screamed and ran away.

"Get me out! Squeaky!" Squeaky came down and pried open the cage, and we both ran up to the tree as fast as we could. We jumped through the trees till we came to where all the boys were.

The little boy was standing in front of them, telling a wild story of how the giant snake nearly swallowed him whole and how he barely made it out alive. He was the campground hero; the troupe leader was pinning a bravery badge on him in front of all the kids. I just sat there thinking how great it was being a boy and how I missed it so. I looked down one last time at the little boy. He was looking right at me, smiling and waving goodbye. I'd never been so happy to be caught in a cage as I did that day.

CHAPTER 15

Solace's Choice

Meanwhile back at Mr. Lapin's, Solace was pacing back and forth. "It's been days. What do I do, Mr. Lapin? Do I keep waiting or try to make it home? Should I go look for them?"

"Child, I really think if they were gonna return, they'd be here by now. If Pibby hasn't found him by now, something must have gone wrong. I'm so sorry." Mr. Lapin sighed.

Solace fell to her knees crying. "They did this for me!" Solace lay down and cried herself to sleep.

Mr. Lapin, knowing he was in no shape to try to take her home, decided to go to the falls to ask his friends for their advice. Maybe someone would offer their help. Making sure Solace was asleep, he headed to the falls. When he arrived, the raccoons and a few birds were in the water, cooling off.

"Hello, Mr. Lapin," the birds sang in unison. The raccoons just nodded and went on bathing in the cool water of the spring.

"I come here to find help for the princess of the grove. We must get her back home."

"Where are Pibby and Squeaky?" the birds sang.

"I'm afraid they met their end while trying to deliver the princess."

"No!" the gator said, poking his head up out of the water.

"What's wrong with everybody?" two deer asked, walking up.

Before long, everyone at the falls had heard the terrible news. "We must complete their task for them!" everyone answered.

"Who's gonna offer to take her to the rest of the way?" Mr. Lapin asked.

"I will!" Sova said, landing at the water's edge. Everyone scattered back into the bushes. "Come out!" Sova said. "I'm not gonna harm anyone! I helped Pibby to the gorge where the hawks had Squeaky. Then I saved them from the hawks and hid in the barn till they had time to slip in the stream in a boat they built. They were fine when I last saw them."

Mr. Lapin was the first to return to the falls. "Why should we trust you after all you've done to us?" he asked.

"Pibby showed me what it's like to have friends and to trust someone. I've started eating from fields and gardens, leaving the likes of you alone. Friends are hard to come by," he said. "I kinda like not being alone all the time."

By this time, all the animals had creeped back to the water's edge.

"How do we know this isn't a trick just to get the princess?"

"Pibby is my friend, and any friend of his is mine also. The hawks are still looking for them, so we need to get her out of here soon," Sova said. "I can't fight them all. I can fly her to the grove in a day's time, where she'll be safe."

"I'll have to ask Solace. You meet us back here tomorrow at this time. We'll give you an answer!" Mr. Lapin shouted.

"Good enough!" Sova said, flying off.

"Can we trust him?" everyone asked.

"Well, he didn't eat us!" Lapin said. "It'll be up to the princess. I must get back to her before she wakes up. I'll see you all tomorrow. Bring everyone with you tomorrow." Mr. Lapin hurried back to his hole and found Solace sleeping in the same place he left her. *I let her sleep. She has a big decision to make tomorrow.*

Mr. Lapin went to his shop and started on making a harness for Solace to wear. Sova could grab the harness instead of her. He took some leather and sewed it together. It kinda looked like a vest with two big loops on top of each shoulder. About the time he was finishing it, Solace walked in from sleeping.

"What's that your making?" she asked.

"Well, it's for you, dear."

"Me? Leather is really not my style, Mr. Lapin." She laughed. "I'm more of a prissy kinda lady. I like big dresses and fancy hats."

"Try it on anyway, please?" Mr. Lapin asked.

"Well, okay, but I'm telling you, I won't like it. What's this loop on the shoulders for?"

"So that something or somebody can carry you."

"What do you mean carry me?"

"I built this so a bird could carry you to your home in the grove tomorrow. He can get you there in a day's time. What do you think about that, Ms. Solace?" Lapin asked.

"Carry me way above the trees, dangling in this leather vest? I don't think so! I would rather walk home," she said.

"Too dangerous, you see, the hawks are the ones that took Squeaky, and they're still searching for you three."

"You three! You mean they're still alive?"

"We think so. They were last seen headed downstream on the boat y'all built. We must get you home as soon as possible so the guardians can protect you. Pibby and Squeaky are on the stream that goes right through the grove. Don't you wanna be there when they arrive?" Lapin asked her.

"Well, yeah, but on a bird? What bird agreed to do this for me anyway?"

"You'll meet him tomorrow at the falls. He assured us that you'll be safe." Mr. Lapin didn't want to spring Sova's name on her tonight. She wouldn't sleep a wink.

Solace walked back into the hole and found something to eat. Mr. Lapin stayed in the shop to make Solace some type of long spear so she could fight off predators if attacked. He hoped he was making the right decision. He would sure hate to let Pibby down after he had saved his life earlier.

He fashioned the spear out of a long straight limb. Then he whittled it down so she could handle it easy. Who knows, she may have to poke Sova a time or two with it.

*****

89

Mr. Lapin didn't sleep a wink that night, worrying about Solace's decision tomorrow. He woke up first the next morning. Solace woke up a little later and fixed them a small breakfast of berries and carrots.

Solace packed her things and threw them over her back and looked at Mr. Lapin and said, "Just in case!"

They left the hole and headed for the falls, not in any hurry because they were really early. She stopped to pick flowers along the way. With the knowledge of Squeaky and Pibby still alive, it lifted her spirits. They arrived at the falls, and it was full of animals of every kind. Birds of every kind were singing. Deer were up to their bellies in the water. Ducks were swimming under the falls to cool off. Even a pig had managed to make himself a mud puddle to wallow in. Everyone was talking, singing, and playing until she walked up. Then there was dead silence.

"It's the princess!" everyone said at once.

"Princess! I'm no princess! Just a common squirrel girl!" They weren't buying it. The blue eyes she had were giving her away. She was special, and they knew it. Solace laid her stuff down and jumped in headfirst. She jumped up and said, "See! A common squirrel girl!"

Everybody laughed, but they still weren't buying it.

"I don't see a bird here big enough to carry me anywhere!" Solace said to Mr. Lapin.

"He'll be here shortly."

An hour or so went by, and with a big swoop, Sova landed on the edge of the falls. Solace screamed and tried to get out of the water.

"It's okay. It's okay. He's friendly!" they all shouted.

"Friendly my behind!" Solace shouted. "Y'all didn't hear what he told us back in the forest! He all but told us if he saw us again, we'd be his dinner."

"Things have changed. Pibby showed me what it could be like to have friends. I helped him find Squeaky, then saved them from the hawks. I really want to help you get home, Ms. Solace. It's getting dangerous to stay here. The hawks are spreading out looking for the three of you," Sova said.

"So I'm supposed to trust you with my life?"

"I will guard it with mine. I owe that much to Pibby."

PIBBY'S ADVENTURES

Everyone at the falls was waiting on Solace's answer. "It's the only way!" everyone started saying. "We want you to make it home, princess."

Mr. Lapin handed her the spear he made her and said, "You can poke him and anyone that bothers you on the way."

"And I will, bird! If you look at me the wrong way, I'll shove this to you know where!" she said.

"Yes, ma'am!" Sova shouted.

"Hooray!" everyone shouted.

Mr. Lapin said, "Get your vest on. We've wasted enough time already."

Solace hugged Mr. Lapin, thanked everyone, and said, "I'm ready, bird!"

Sova grabbed her by the loops, and they were off.

"Hooray! Hooray! Goodbye, princess!"

CHAPTER 16

A Horse's Tale

Squeaky was moving fast to get away from the campground.

"Slow down!" I said. "We're out of danger!" I didn't really know that, but I was tired. I couldn't get that little boy out of my mind. It kept going through my mind. What would I do if I had the choice to go back? I miss my family, but I wouldn't want to leave this family either. Who knows, this still may be the longest dream ever. If it was, it sure didn't feel it. *Whatever!* I thought to myself. *I'm in it, so I'll just go with it.*

Squeaky grabbed my arm and got my attention. He pointed up ahead at some commotion going on.

"Hit the trees!" I shouted.

Like before, we snuck up on them through the trees. When we got to where all the movement was, we noticed a small horse who had fallen in old abandon hole. He was trying his best to get out but couldn't quite make it out. He would get to the edge, and it would collapse, and he would fall back in. From the looks of the hole, he had been here for a while.

We crawled down the tree to where he was and said, "Looks like you need some help, fellow." It was just a foal.

"I can't get out of here!" he said.

"Where's your mom? Why are you here all alone?" I asked.

"A fox ran us through the forest, and we got separated. It's been a day or so since I saw her. Please get me out!" he said.

"Okay, first of all, what's your name? I'm Pibby. This is Squeaky."

"Hindi is my name. My mom and I have been on our own since I was born."

Now I had no idea how to get a horse out of a hole. "Let me think," I said. We weren't big or strong enough to pull a log to the hole or anything like that. "All we can do is dig down the side low enough that you can get out."

"That'll take forever!" Squeaky said.

"We can't leave him in there!" I said.

"I got it!" Squeaky said. "Hindi, start pulling down the side of the wall into the bottom of the hole. When you get a lot pulled down, start stomping it down to build up the bottom of the hole."

Hindi did what Squeaky said, and it looked like it was working. Hindi's head seemed to be rising on the side he was working. He finally got it high enough where he thought he could jump out.

"Okay, stand back!" He backed up as far as he could, ran, and jumped as hard as he could; and *wham*, he was out.

"Alright! Good job, Hindi!" we both said.

"Ah, it feels so good to be out!" He jumped all around like a newborn colt. "I feel like running! Where you guys headed? I'll run you anywhere you wanna go!" Hindi shouted.

I looked at Squeaky and said, "Why not? Beats walking!"

We jumped up on Hindi and said, "Go east, buddy."

He started walking, and I said, "The other east."

"Sorry, I don't know what east is."

"Hold on! We're gonna run awhile!" Hindi took off, running as fast as he could. We held on to his mane, laughing the whole time.

We really didn't know where we were or where we were heading. East was the right direction; we knew that much. Hindi slowed down to a walk after a while and would stop to eat berries when he saw them. I hoped we would come across his mom on the trail. He was too young to be on his own. The fox he was talking about concerned me also. Could it be Roka? We couldn't be that close to the grove. Roka wasn't the only fox in these forests, so it could've been anyone.

The trail opened up to where there was barely a tree in sight. Now we really had to keep our eyes peeled for predators. No sooner than I thought it, a big red fox appeared behind us.

"Run, Hindi! Run!" I shouted.

Hindi ran as fast as he could toward the biggest hill in front of him. The fox was dead on his butt, nipping at his tail. The hill was slowing Hindi down.

Squeaky said, "Hold on to me!" He grabbed his bow and was shooting the fox in the face. It had no effect on the fox. He grabbed Hindi's leg for a moment, and Hindi pulled away.

I knew I had to do something, or Hindi and we were goners. I pulled my sword, ran down Hindi's back, and jumped toward the fox. When I landed on the fox sword first, I drove it deep in his neck. He started tumbling, throwing me to the ground. Pain was running down my whole body. I couldn't move.

The fox landed on top of me, not moving. I tried pushing him off, but he was too heavy. Hindi was still running as fast as he could away from me. Squeaky tried to stop him but couldn't. They kept getting farther and farther away. An hour later, I was still lying there. Everything was quiet, and I was getting weaker. I lay there looking up at the sky, and suddenly, I saw Sova, and he had Solace. How did he find her? Why was he going back on our deal? I thought we were friends.

They disappeared into the forest. I was so mad that I didn't realize I had wiggled my way out from under the fox. My leg was hurt, but I didn't know how bad. I tried standing up, but it hurt too bad. There was a hill nearby. I knew I had to get in some cover before scavengers came for this fox.

Dragging myself to the nearest boulder, I dug a hole behind it and lay down to hide. Surely Squeaky would be back to get me. Lying there, all I could think about was Solace. The worse thing was there was nothing I could do to help her.

Dark was fast approaching, so I pulled the branches and leaves over me for the night. Was this how it all ends? How bad was I hurt? Was Solace and Squeaky alright? I had a million questions going through my mind.

There were growling noises coming from the body of the fox. The scavengers had found it and were fighting over it. I wasn't very far away from them. *Hope they don't pick up my scent and come over*

PIBBY'S ADVENTURES

here. They stayed all night with the body, so sleeping was out of the question. Finally, I just passed out from the pain and exhaustion.

"Pibby! Pibby!" was the first thing I heard waking up the next morning. Squeaky had finally got Hindi to stop and made the long trek back to me. I crawled out of my hole and shouted, "Over here!"

Squeaky came running and kneeling down beside me. "You okay?"

"My leg, I think it's broken," I said.

"Let me see." Squeaky looked at it and said, "It's broken. We need two sticks and some rope to make a splint for it. Hold on, I'll go find some."

"Don't worry, I'll be right here," I said with a grin.

Hindi walked over and said, "Thanks for saving me again. I thought we were done for. We'll be back on the trail shortly."

"Hopefully, we'll find your mom on the way," I told him.

Squeaky got my leg ready for travel, and he helped me up on Hindi's back, and we were off again. I told Squeaky what I saw, and we headed in the direction I saw them go.

We were on the trail a few hours, and Hindi suddenly stopped in his tracks. "My mom was here. I can smell where she stood. She went that way."

He turned to go left, and I said, "That's not the way we need to go though."

Hindi said, "I got to find her!"

"What do we do? We can't send him by himself to find her." I looked at Squeaky.

He shrugged his shoulders and said, "Why not? We have been everywhere else on this trip, might as well do this."

"Okay. Hindi, follow your nose, buddy. We'll help you find your mom," I said, shaking my head.

He took off to the left with his nose in the air. The forest completely ended about a mile after we turned. It turned to an open pasture for as far as we could see.

"She walked this way! See!"

We saw hoofprints headed across the pasture land, and we started following them. All I could think was that we're getting farther and farther away from Solace. All of a sudden, Hindi bucked both Squeaky and me to the ground and took off across the pasture. Looking way across the pasture, we could see a giant horse running this way.

Squeaky said, "I hope she knows we're his buddies."

"Me too!" I said, laughing.

Hindi's mom was a huge beautiful horse with a long flowing mane. Hindi told her how we saved him and rescued him from the hole. She thanked us and asked what she could do to help.

"Just give us a ride back to the trail, and we'll make it from there," I said. I really didn't know how we would make it from there, but I couldn't ask them to risk themselves for us any longer.

She agreed, and we climbed back up on Hindi and headed back. It was getting late, and we still had a way to go to get back to the trail.

Hindi's mom told us about an old barn just across from where we were that we could stay the night. The barn was just big enough for Hindi's mom to stand up in. We climbed down and found a good place in the corner to lie down. Hindi and his mom walked over to the other side and lay down beside each other.

My leg wasn't hurting as bad anymore. Squeaky did a great job wrapping it. I looked over at Hindi sleeping and looked back at Squeaky and said, "Let's get up before them and leave. They've been through enough."

Squeaky agreed, and we drifted off to sleep. Solace was the last thing on my mind as I went to sleep. We woke up about an hour before daylight and slipped out, leaving them sleeping in the barn. I found a stick and used it as a crutch to help me walk. It felt like we were getting close, but neither one of us knew for sure.

CHAPTER 17

Solace's Flight

"Whoa! I should've thought about this a little more! Do you have to fly so high and fast?" Solace shouted at Sova. Solace looked back at the animals as the falls got smaller and smaller. It was too late to turn back now. She really wanted to get home and see her dad and friends.

Solace's dad was really protective over her since they lost her mother. She didn't want for much living in the grove. Everything was at her fingertips, and her dad saw to it. Solace was the only female squirrel with blue eyes. That was because her mom was a changer like Pibby. No one knew where her mom came from; she just showed up one day. The grove took her in, and the rest was history. Solace couldn't get her mind off Pibby though. Maybe he'd be in the grove when they arrive.

Sova flew over a wide-open pasture, and Solace saw a dead fox lying in the middle of it. "Well, that's not a good sign!" she said out loud.

They flew most of the day till Sova said, "I'm gonna land and rest for a while. I'll sit you down in the top of that big tree over there, Ms. Solace."

"Very well, bird," she answered. Sova sat her down and landed in the tree next to her. Solace opened her bag and started eating some berries.

"I'm gonna fly over to that pond just over that hill and catch a fish to eat. I'll be right back," Sova said, flying off.

"Okay, don't be too long. I'm ready to get home!"

Sova disappeared over the hill and dove for the first fish he saw. Catching it, he flew to the nearest bank and started eating it. He had eaten most of it and was about to take off when two hawks landed on top of him, pinning him to the ground. Three more hawks landed on the bank beside Sova.

"All we wanna know is where you left this so-called princess. We're working for someone who really wants her back. Now tell us where she is, and you'll survive this!" the hawks shouted.

"Never gonna happen! Who could possibly want a little lady squirrel?" Sova asked.

"She was stolen from him, and he wants her back. You might as well tell us. We'll find her anyway." Sova didn't answer. "Very well, break his wings. We want him to die slowly."

Two hawks spread Sova's wings as far as they would go. The other two grabbed the biggest rocks they could lift and flew above Sova. They dropped the rocks at the same time. The rocks hit Sova's wings at the same time, breaking them both. Sova screeched with pain so loud that Solace heard him and knew something was wrong.

She crawled down the tree to find a hole she could get in. The tree next to her had one, so she jumped to the tree and scurried into the hole. Sova screeched as loud as he could again. He was in a lot of pain, but that wasn't the reason he was being so loud. The hawks let him up and flew up to a tree above Sova.

"All you had to do is tell us where she was, and you wouldn't die out here alone. Oh, well, we have a princess to find!" the hawks said, flying away.

Solace peeked out of the hole and saw the hawks circling above her. She moved to the back of the hole and lay down. Wait was all she could do now. The hawks would move on when they won't find her. She lay there wondering what they did to Sova. *I'll go check in the morning*, she thought to herself.

Sova waded into the pond to ease the pain. He knew he couldn't survive long like this. If only Pibby was here to fix his wings again. He walked out of the water to a hillside cave and went inside. Propped

PIBBY'S ADVENTURES

up beside the cave wall, he passed out from the pain. Surely this would be his final resting place.

They both were asleep and not sure if this was their last day on this earth. Did fate lead them here or would fate keep them alive?

The next morning, Solace woke up and made sure there weren't any hawks in the area before going out. She didn't see or hear any, so she climbed down the tree and slowly made her way toward the pond where Sova said he was going. The whole time, she was bracing herself for what she may find. The thought of being alone out here scared her.

The pond wasn't very big at all. She walked around it, looking for signs of Sova. "Hey, bird!" she shouted out. No response. Solace could tell he had been there by the marks on the ground. She decided to follow them to see if it might lead her to him.

The tracks went away from the pond toward the hill behind her. They led her to the cave where Sova lay motionless against the wall. Sova had never woke up that morning. Solace stood there with tears streaming down her face, thinking, *He died helping me*, feeling ashamed that she never gave him the respect he deserved. Sova had died with something that he had never had in his life, friends.

Solace started piling rocks at the little cave's entrance so no scavengers could find his body. It took her most of the day to finish, but he deserved at least this much, she thought. She would stop and cry for a little while and then work. After she finished, she made her way back to the hole she had stayed in last night. Solace lay down and cried herself to sleep. She felt ashamed of the way she treated Sova, but all that was too late now.

The morning came with more crying, but she knew she had to get on the trail home. What she didn't know was how she was gonna do it. She never had to do it on her own. Solace packed her things, threw her sack over her shoulder, and climbed down the tree. She decided to keep going the way Sova was flying; it had to be the right direction.

The morning was kinda rainy, and the wind was picking up. The faster she walked, the faster she'd get there. She was thinking out loud, "Oh, how I wish Squeaky and Pibby are here. I hope they're okay."

It rained most of the day, but she never stopped, determined to make it to the grove. Suddenly, she heard hawks screeching in the skies above, so Solace went tree to tree, looking up and listening for them. It was slow, but it's better than getting caught. If she knew the emperor, he'd be bringing the whole crew. That's why she had to keep moving. She didn't know how far behind her they were. There was no stopping now, not even at night. Solace was as scared as she'd ever been, but they'd have to kill her to take her back.

CHAPTER 18

Roka's Revenge

My leg turned out not to be broken. It kept getting better the more I walked on it. We started making good time after I threw the crutch away. Squeaky and I was looking for any sign of Sova and Solace. I still couldn't believe he would do that. Squeaky never trusted him even after he saved our lives.

I could see a small pond up ahead. We figured we'd stop to cool off and take a short break. *Might help to soak my leg in the water for a while*, I thought. The pond water was cool from the recent rain shower.

Squeaky dove underwater and came up on the other side of the pond. "Looks like there were some birds here not long ago!" Squeaky shouted.

"Probably doing the same thing we're doing," I said.

"Squirrel prints also! It's a local watering hole, I'm guessing!" he said.

We hung around for a while and decided to get back on the trail. Squeaky followed the tracks up the hill. "Hey, the squirrel and bird went the same way!"

"What?" I ran up to him and saw what he was talking about. The tracks led up to the hill and then came to a small cave that had been rocked up. "What in the world!" I asked.

"Looks like a grave to me!" Squeaky answered.

"Pibby, Pibby," I heard someone calling my name where I could barely hear them.

"It's coming from the cave!" Squeaky shouted.

We started pulling away the rocks as fast as we could.

"Sova!" Squeaky pulled his bow back and aimed for Sova's head.

"Hold on!" I said. "He's hurt pretty bad. Where's Solace!" I shouted at him. "What did you do to her!"

"Let me shoot him!" Squeaky shouted.

Sova whispered as loud as he could, "The hawks did this to me. I was flying her home, and we stopped to rest, and they ambushed me at the pond. Solace was back in the trees when it happened. She came after they left, and she must have thought I was dead 'cause she blocked up the entrance to the cave."

"What did they do to you?" I asked.

"Broke both my wings. I guess I passed out. I'm sorry I let her down," Sova said.

"Squeaky, go bring some water and something for him to eat. We got to splint his wings again."

Squeaky ran down to the pond and filled his canteen and brought it to Sova. He took some carrots and berries out of his bag and gave them to him also.

"The hawks are working for the emperor. He's after Solace."

"The emperor? I shot him back in the city," Squeaky said.

"That's what they said, that he wants her back and is coming after her," Sova said.

"Okay! We've got to hurry! Squeaky grabbed his wing and pulled it out straight."

When Squeaky pulled his wing, it made a loud *pop*, and Sova let out a loud screech. Sova slowly started moving his wing.

"Hey! I think they just dislocated it. It's sore, but it will move."

Squeaky moved around to the other wing and yanked on it. *Screech!* And Sova passed out on the ground. "Guess this one was broken!" Squeaky said.

"Hold it there. I'll put the splint on it." After we had the splint on, I said, "Squeaky, leave your canteen and food. We'll put the rocks back up, and he'll be safe while he heals. We've got to go find Solace before they do!"

PIBBY'S ADVENTURES

After blocking the cave entrance back up, we took off, trying to pick up her trail. The tree she stayed in was easy to locate because her prints led right to it. After that, the rain pretty much washed them away. But we could tell what direction she was headed. It rained off and on the whole day. All I could think about was her going back to that city. There's no way we could save her a second time; we barely did it the first time.

It got late, and we decided to keep moving, hoping to gain some ground on her. Maybe she stopped and rested for the night. We traveled most of the night and finally stopped to rest in this old dead hollow stump.

"Let's stay here till the sun comes up, and we'll get back on it." It won't help if we're too tired to help her if we find her.

We curled up in the stump, listening to the rain fall. I was thinking, *Solace must be scared to death out here by herself.* Sleep didn't come easy, but I finally drifted off.

The rain had stopped when we woke up the next morning. After eating something, we got back on the trail. We came to a clearing in the forest, and Squeaky said, "Stop!"

"What is it, Squeaky?"

"I know this place. It's right outside the grove! We're almost to the far end of the grove!"

"No way!" I said.

"Yes, sir! By the end of the day, we'll be at the edge of the grove," Squeaky said.

"It's too bad you almost made it home!" a voice from the bushes said. "It's a shame, all that trouble you went through just for it to end right here! What a sad story it will be. Heroes die trying to save the princess."

"Roka!" Squeaky whispered to me. "Let's go!"

We started to run off, and Roka said, "No, no, no! I've got something you want!" Roka walked out of the bushes, and he had Solace in his mouth. He dropped her on the ground in front of him. "I kept her alive, knowing you two would be along shortly! And here you are, the two tricksters. You know I hung from that tree for two days!" Roka shouted.

103

"So what do you want!" I shouted.

He picked Solace up and said, "Follow me, boys!"

We had no choice but to follow. One bite down and Solace would be dead. He came to a cliff that looked down over sharp jagged rocks below. "Climb out to the end of that limb, both of you!" Roka had stuck a long limb out over the edge of the cliff and piled rocks on one end of it.

We walked out to the end of the limb and turned around. "Now what!" I said.

"I put you out there to make sure you don't pull any tricks. All I have to do is kick this stone off this end and to the rocks below you fall," Roka answered.

"What about Solace?" Squeaky shouted.

"I hear someone is trading ten fat squirrels for this one scrawny little blue-eyed one. I figured I would stay here till he showed up!" Roka said.

"Emperor!" I said to Squeaky.

"Yeah! That's what they called him! Said he was crazy about this little chick. They said she was gonna be his wife back in the big city, and two pesky squirrels ruined his wedding day. Y'all wouldn't know anything about that, would you? I figure I might get at least twenty squirrels for her and you two," Roka said, laughing. "Now don't go falling off and ruining my merchandise. He should be here by tomorrow. Get comfortable, boys."

We sat down and looked down at the rocks below us. The fall would kill us, not to mention the rocks. I couldn't see any way out. This really could be the way it all ends.

Roka lay down at the end of the log with Solace between him and the cliff. She was still unconscious and lying there wet from Roka's saliva.

"Sova can't save us. He can't fly."

"I can shoot him!"

"He's too big, Squeaky," I said.

Needless to say, we weren't sleeping anytime soon. I couldn't believe we made it this far and this close to home, and it was over.

PIBBY'S ADVENTURES

Solace woke up and saw us on the end of the limb and ran to us. "Oh, I'm so glad to see you two!" She hugged both of us and said, "What does he want with us?"

"He's gonna trade you to the emperor for ten squirrels. Us too!" I said.

"I'll jump before I go back there!" She stood up.

I grabbed her and said, "Just wait! We'll figure a way out." I didn't believe that, but I had to calm her down. We lay there all night, watching Roka sleep. He had his foot resting on the stone, holding the limb up.

*****

The emperor showed up with his cat guard and thirty or more squirrels tied hand to hand. Tonito and his crew from the city, they must have captured them all when we broke Solace out.

"Well, what do we have here? This is better than I dreamed of! My princess and my two biggest enemies. And it's not even my birthday!"

Roka said, "I want twenty squirrels for the three of them."

"Heck, man, you can have all of them! I'm tired of feeding them," the emperor said. "Now come over here, my blue-eyed beauty! We have a wedding we didn't quite finish!"

"I'll never go back!" Solace shouted. She moved to the edge of the limb and said, "I'll jump before I go back!"

"You'll never do that. You like yourself too much!" the emperor said.

Solace had her back to the drop and just fell off backward. Squeaky and I shouted, "No!" and reached to grab her, but it was too late; she was gone. The emperor's face dropped in disbelief. I bent over in pain.

When I bent over, I saw Sova and Solace standing at the bottom of the cliff. Trying not to give it away, I stayed bent over, acting like I was still in pain. Squeaky drew his bow and pointed it at Roka.

"All I have to do is move this rock, and you're goners with your little princess. Now put the bow down!" Roka said.

105

"Jump!" I whispered to Squeaky. "Sova will catch you."

Squeaky glanced down and saw Sova. "You first!" he whispered back.

I said, "What the heck. I can't live without her!" I fell face-first, and Sova wrapped his wing around me as I reached the bottom.

Roka couldn't believe it. "Cowards! They're just giving up!"

"Not so fast!" the emperor said out loud. He ran over to the edge and saw us at the bottom. "I knew it! Call the hawks in! Send the cat patrol around to the bottom."

Squeaky jumped about that time and pulled his bow at the same time. He let a shot off and nipped the emperor's ear. Squeaky grinned at him while falling down to Sova's clutch. We had a pretty good lead on the emperor's crew.

I led them through the bottom of the canyon. By the time Roka and the cat patrol could make it down there, we'd be deep in the forest. Sova couldn't fly, but he could keep up with his legs. He was telling me which way to go as we entered the edge of the forest. I didn't know where we were headed, but I trusted Sova completely now.

Back at the cliff, the emperor was gathering all his crew and about thirty hawks. "I want them found and brought to me. Do not harm the princess!" he demanded.

"What do you want to do with these squirrel prisoners?" Roka asked.

"Tie them to the trees on the edge of the cliff. You can have them when you bring me the princess!" the emperor shouted.

The emperor's crew tied Tonito's crew from the city to the trees lining the cliff's edge. The hawks took off toward the forest, spreading out to cover more ground. The cat patrol started the long trek around to get to the bottom. The emperor was leading the pack, barking orders as he led.

*****

In the forest, our crowd was moving fast and following Sova's directions. It was getting late, and we hadn't slowed down a bit. We came to the stream's edge, and Sova said, "That's the edge of the grove around that bend."

About that time, Pesco poked his head out of the water and said, "Thought I never see y'all again!"

"Well, it's good to see you again!" I said.

"He's gonna carry y'all into the grove as far as he can. It's getting shallow, so we don't exactly know how far he can go. I'll keep going this way to throw them off your trail," Sova said.

"Pesco, you ate anything lately?" Solace asked, laughing.

"I'm full as I can be!" he said.

Solace hugged Sova and started crying. "I thought you were dead. Thank you so much for saving us."

I patted him on the shoulder and said, "You're doing that a lot lately!"

Squeaky walked by him and said, "Thanks."

"We better go!" Pesco shouted. "It's getting late."

"We'll see you later, Sova, I promise!" I said.

Solace hugged him one more time and said bye. With that, we all stepped in Pesco's mouth, and he slowly went under and headed upstream toward the grove.

Sova took off back down the trail. Solace was holding my hand as hard as she could with her head on my shoulder. My heart was beating a thousand times a minute. Not because I was in a big fish's mouth, but it was because I was loving who I was with.

Pesco swam upstream for about an hour or so, then pulled to the bank. "This is it! As far as I can go!"

We jumped out and thanked him a thousand times, and he turned and said, "I'll stay around this area if you need me in the next couple days."

*****

Roka and the emperor stopped right after dark and set up camp. The hawks stayed in the trees above them. Altogether, the emperor had about eighty in his crew and thirty hawks.

"We will catch her tomorrow! Whoever catches them will be in charge of the crew from now on!"

Roka said, "All I want is the two pesky ones! I should have eaten them when I had my chance."

They all sat around fires and ate whatever they could find.

*****

I led them to a big hole way up a big cypress tree, and we all collapsed on the floor.

"We're in the grove, but I'm not sure exactly where," Squeaky said.

"We'll figure it out in the morning. We need to help Tonito's crew escape after we take Solace to her father," I whispered.

Solace had drifted off to sleep already. Her safety was the most important thing to me now.

Squeaky said, "The whole grove is in danger now! We've got to warn everyone!"

I agreed, saying, "We're gonna have to put an end to the emperor's crew before he'll leave us alone. The guardians will know what to do."

"We just have to make it there first!" Squeaky sighed.

We didn't say another word for the rest of the night. Solace still had my hand, and I pulled her closer and went to sleep. Meanwhile, Mr. Lapin had been watching from a hill across the cliff edge.

CHAPTER 19

Homecoming

Mr. Lapin followed Sova to the cliffs and stayed back on the opposite side to spy on the emperor. He and Sova planned to meet up after Sova led the general's crew away from me. Mr. Lapin had watched them tie up Tonito's bunch and just left one guard with them. He had to figure out a way to free them and get rid of the guard.

The birds from the falls had come with Mr. Lapin along with a few other of his friends. Mr. Lapin sent all the birds to land in the trees above Tonito's crew. The raccoon was sent to climb the cliff behind Tonito. The birds' job was to get the cat guards' attention while the raccoon untied Tonito's crew.

Singing and making as much noise as they could, the birds plan was working. The cat guard walked down to the last tree, looking up at the birds and said, "Come down a little closer, and one of you will be my dinner tonight!"

While this was happening, the raccoon was cutting all the crew members loose. About ten crew were loose and were planning to ambush the cat guard. One crew member climbed the tree behind the cat and dropped the heaviest rock he could find on his head. The cat guard fell; the rest jumped on him and proceeded to tie him up. The rest of the crew members were loose at this point, waiting on instructions from Tonito.

Mr. Lapin had made it around by now and was introducing himself to Tonito. He asked him if he and his crew would wait around for Sova to see what the next move would be.

"I'd do anything to help Pibby and Squeaky and to get rid of the emperor once and for all," Tonito answered.

"Sova should be back in the morning. Tell your crew to make camp on the cliff opposite of this one. There will be plenty food for everyone over there already," Mr. Lapin said.

They all made their way to the camp and put guards on each entrance.

*****

I woke up first and peeked outside. Everything was clear, so I went and gathered some food for everyone and went back to the hole. Solace was waking up when I crawled back in the entrance. "Good morning, sleepyhead!" I said.

That woke Squeaky up, and we all ate what I had gathered for them.

"I think we should try to make it to Mr. Mudar's before the night. At least it'll be a good hiding place. Mr. Mudar will know the best thing to do," Squeaky said.

"You just wanna eat some of his food and swim in his pond!" I said jokingly.

"That too!" Squeaky laughed.

"Pond?" Solace asked.

"Yes, ma'am, he has a built-in pond in his hole!" I said.

"Don't threaten me with a good time!" Solace laughed.

"We'll have to figure out where we are exactly. Y'all two have lived here all your lives, so surely you'll notice something sooner or later. We'll figure it out as we go," I said.

Squeaky stood up and said, "Pack up and let's get going!"

We all packed up, and out of the hole we went. The direction away from where the emperor was seemed like the smartest way to start. We all agreed on that decision. Solace was excited at the idea of

PIBBY'S ADVENTURES

being home and seeing her dad. She also was wondering whether this thing with me was real or was it just this task I was doing.

Solace grabbed my hand. I looked back and smiled at her and squeezed her hand. We all sensed a safer feeling now that we were in a familiar territory.

"Look!" Squeaky shouted. "That's the opening where Roka almost killed Pibby!"

"Well, don't be so happy about it!" I said.

"You know what I mean. We should hit the trees, and we could make it to Mr. Mudar's place by dark," Squeaky said.

We climbed up and started jumping from tree to tree. I missed a few times and had to climb back up to catch up.

"You're not too good at this tree-jumping thing, are you?" Solace laughed.

"I get it from my brother. He fell out every tree he ever climbed!" We all laughed out loud.

The next hours flew by, and by dust, we were knocking on Mr. Mudar's door.

"Coming! Hold onto your britches!" A few minutes later, he opened the door to see the three of us standing there. "Well, this is the most glorious sight I've ever seen in all my years! I had given up on all of you. Matter of fact, the whole grove has! It is so good to see your little young faces." He proceeded to hug everyone.

"I know you're tired and hungry, so make yourself at home, and I'll rustle up some groceries!"

"We need to tell you something!" I said.

"We can discuss it over dinner. Y'all go jump in the pond and freshen up." He didn't have to say that but once. We were on our way before he got through saying it.

Jumping in headfirst, Squeaky yelled, "We made it home!"

Solace and I were next to jump in. I thought it was the most relaxed I'd ever been in my life. We laughed and kidded around with each other till we heard, "Dinner's ready!" Mr. Mudar shouted down the hall.

The table was loaded with all kinds of fruits and vegetables. Mr. Mudar handed me a bowl and said, "Here, just for you!" The bowl was filled with freshly picked butter beans.

111

I smiled and felt tears fill my eyes 'cause it made me think of home. We ate till we could hardly breathe.

"The grove is in danger. We have to warn everyone!" I said. "There's this whole crew coming for Solace, and he won't let anything stop him from getting her. He followed us back from the city and brought all his cat guards with him."

"You must tell the guardians first," Mr. Mudar said. "Everyone will be warned soon enough. It's too dangerous tonight, so find yourself a place to lay your head tonight. You can leave at first light in the morning."

We all slept in the same room, guess we felt safer altogether now. I grabbed Solace's hand and told her, "Almost home, lady." She hugged me and closed her eyes. I think we slept better that night than the past month.

Leaving the house the next morning wasn't easy. Mr. Mudar packed us a lunch and said, "I'll be coming behind you in the next few days."

Squeaky led like usual, and we followed close behind. Squeaky knew where he was going now, so we were making good time. Trouble was we didn't know how much time we actually had. Did Sova lead them away far enough for us to get to the guardians? For all we know, they could be right behind us.

The guardians lived in the three biggest trees in the grove. It was their job to keep the grove safe. This job may be too hard for anyone though. The emperor had the advantage of all his crew being cats. They were natural hunters and excellent at killing things. We were just a bunch of squirrels, turtles, and rabbits.

We arrived at the guardians' lair after a few hours. Solace immediately ran to her dad and hugged him. All three guardians were out on their perches when we arrived.

Squeaky's dad walked up to Squeaky and said, "I was wrong about you. You made me a proud dad. I've been told of all your heroics and bravery, how you escaped danger and saved your friends life."

"I couldn't have done it without Pibby's help. He saved my life several times," Squeaky said.

PIBBY'S ADVENTURES

"We had lots of friends that helped along the way, but we're not out of trouble! The grove is in trouble. Someone is coming for Solace, and he has lots of friends with him."

Solace was still close to her dad and saw the concern in his face. "What kind of friends does this intruder have with him?" the black guardian asked.

"Cats!" Solace answered. "A lot of them!"

"We had a friend leading them on a wild-goose chase, but they'll be back. We must warn all the animals in the grove!"

"There's no way we can stop that many cats," the guardian said.

"There may be!" I said. "We've got friends that he has tied up just out of the grove. Squeaky and I will go free them while y'all warn the grove. We'll try to make them chase us away from the grove."

"Okay, we'll come your way once we've warned everyone."

"What about me?" Solace shouted.

CHAPTER 20

The Battle

Solace was told not to leave home for any reason by her father. Squeaky and I headed toward the cliff where Tonito's crew were captive. The guardians were spreading out to warn the grove of the pending danger. Solace was pouting at home. Sova was circling back to the cliff also.

Squeaky and I showed up before Sova, and we were surprised to see Mr. Lapin and the freed Tonito crew. Mr. Lapin filled us in on Sova's plan to circle back to the cliff.

"We've got to lead them away from the grove somehow!" I said. "Tonito, have you got a girl on your crew?"

"Yep, but she is tougher than your normal squirrel," he said.

"Good!" I said. "We'll dress her like Solace, and they'll think she's still with us."

"We don't have to, she's right there," Squeaky said.

Solace came walking up and said, "If you think you're leaving me at home, you're crazy!"

"Your dad ain't gonna be happy about this!" Squeaky laughed.

I just stood there shaking my head. "We're still gonna use your girl, Tonito, if that's alright?"

"She said it's okay with her," Tonito answered.

"Solace, find a change of clothes that don't look so girlish. We don't need you sticking out like a sore thumb."

"What's a thumb?" she asked.

PIBBY'S ADVENTURES

"Never mind!" I said.

Sova showed up about that time and said, "It won't take them long to figure out which way I went."

"Mr. Lapin, can you make another vest like you made for Solace?" I asked.

"I brought two with me, thinking we might use them. I made some more bows also. They're in a pile over by that tree."

"Okay. Sova, you'll grab the Solace look-alike and fly over the emperor and lead him to the bottom of the cliffs. We'll get on either side and surround them. Tonito, put your crew in the trees on both sides with the bows. The hawks are your responsibility. We'll try to pound the rest with rocks from the cliffs. Sova, come pick me up after you lead them here and dropped the girl off."

Squeaky said, "I'll help with the hawks from the air."

"Okay, but I'm not flying on a healthy wing, just remember," Sova said.

*****

The guardians showed up with about fifty animals. I explained the plan, and we all split up and waited for Sova to lead them to the cliffs. Solace hid from her dad so he wouldn't see her.

"You stay with me!" I told her.

Sova grabbed the fake Solace and flew toward the emperor's crew. The hawks spotted Sova from a good ways. They all screeched loud and headed in his direction.

One shouted down to the emperor, "He's got the princess! Trying to take her to safety!"

"Well, it won't work, bird!" the emperor shouted. "Follow the hawks!" he ordered.

Sova stayed a safe distance from the hawks, ensuring they couldn't catch him. The cat crew was right behind them. I could see Sova coming into the ravine between the cliffs. Sova landed and released the girl and picked up Squeaky. The hawks entered first, and arrows filled the air. A lot of them missed their mark, but some connected and hawks were plummeting to the ground.

115

Sova brought Squeaky in behind them, and he started picking them off one by one. He hardly ever missed his mark. The cat crew made it to the ravine, and the rocks started raining down on them. So much so that they started hiding under boulders. The hawks would grab someone from a tree and drop them to the ground.

This went on for a little while till the hawks' number dwindled dramatically. They all turned and headed toward their home while there was still any left. We had the emperor pinned down in the ravine.

Squeaky told Sova, "Fly me down toward the emperor!" Sova dipped down behind the emperor, and Squeaky's arrow hit his mark, and he fell face-first in the ground.

I stood up on the edge of the cliff and shouted, "Everybody, stop! The emperor's gone! Anyone that won't leave the ravine will suffer the same fate!"

The cat crew and the emperor's crew all came out and made their way back toward the city. Everyone stayed in their positions till they knew it was safe. Sova flew through the ravine, screeching as loud as he could. Squeaky was pumping his fist in the air, screaming, "Yeah!"

I hugged Solace and said, "You're finally safe!"

The guardians stood on the side of the cliff and shouted, "Friends, everyone is invited to a feast in the grove!"

Everyone shouted in unison. We all headed back to the grove, laughing and relieved that it was over. The feast was a spread of any fruit and vegetable you could think of. Music was being played. There was singing, dancing, and hugs all around. The guardians summoned Squeaky and I to their trees and congratulated us on our bravery and sacrifice. They all came out and got everyone's attention.

"We would like to introduce the two newest guardians of the grove, Pibby and Squeaky!"

The crowd all cheered and congratulated us. I turned to hug Solace, and I couldn't find her. "Squeaky, you've seen Solace?"

Squeaky shook his head and went back to talking to his dad. I started looking for her everywhere. Hopefully, she was with a friend in the crowd. And suddenly, it hit me, Roka. I never saw Roka at the

PIBBY'S ADVENTURES

cliffs. I turned to Sova and said, "Did you ever see Roka?" He shook his head no. "Solace is missing!"

Sova instantly took off searching for her from the sky. I told Squeaky. He grabbed his bow and headed for the woods with me. No one noticed us leaving. Sova came back to where we were and said that he saw no signs of her anywhere. "I'll keep looking!" he said.

After Sova took off, Squeaky went one way and I went the other. I walked as far as I could without getting lost myself. As I started back, I heard Solace's scream from somewhere behind me. I ran toward her scream and finally came to where she was.

"Looks like I'm gonna get the prize after all!" Roka shouted. He had Solace by the leg in his mouth.

"Take me instead! I'm the one who made you look like a fool, hanging in that tree like a sack of taters! Then I defeated all your friends and cost you your deal with the emperor. I'm the one you want!"

He slung Solace against a tree, knocking her out cold. "I'll eat her after I'm finished with you!" he shouted as he moved toward me.

I pulled my sword and was determined to end this once and for all. "You've eaten your last squirrel in this grove! You're getting slow and old, and no one is scared of you anymore!" I shouted.

He rushed at me. I moved to the side and cut the side of his face to the bone. Sova landed in the tree above him. I looked over at Solace, and Mr. Mudar was pulling her in the forest behind him.

He rushed again, and I fell on my back, cutting his underside with a long gash. By this time, a large crowd had gathered around us, watching. Squeaky was propped up on a limb above us. Roka rushed toward me, grabbed me, and slung me into a tree. It nearly knocked me out, but I managed to get to my feet.

He came at me again. I jumped up to the tree, and just as he rushed by, I jumped on him sword first. My sword sunk deep in his head, and Roka fell to the ground. Roka didn't move again. Everyone was in dead silence, not believing what they just witnessed. A squirrel was taking down a huge fox. I became a legend that very day.

Solace came rushing out of the woods, hugging me. Squeaky jumped down out of the tree and hugged me too. Everyone started to pat me on the back, saying that was the most amazing thing they'd ever seen. Sova winked at me with those big eyes.

"Let's get back to the feast!" Mr. Mudar shouted.

I wouldn't let go of Solace's arm for the rest of the night. We ate till we all were full, and one by one, everyone said their goodbyes till there were just three of us left.

"What in the world are we gonna do now?"

"Mr. Mudar's pond!"

We all screamed. We arrived at Mr. Mudar's door and knocked. He welcomed us in and said to swim as long as we liked. After swimming all day, we crashed at Mr. Mudar's house for the night.

The next morning, Solace went home and Squeaky and I went to see what our job as guardians of the grove had us doing. Our first duty was to make sure everyone left the grove since the battle yesterday. We started on the border of the grove next to the stream. The stream was the border on one side.

As we were walking by the stream, Pesco popped his head up. "Hey, guys!" he said. "I'm glad I found you. I was hoping I wouldn't have to wait long. Tonito needs our help. The cat crew have them pinned down at the hawks' gorge. Shonta's snake crew is there also."

I said, "We'll go help! I need to find Sova."

"We'll have to get permission from the guardians!" Squeaky shouted.

"I'm leaving now! They were there when we needed them!" I answered.

"I can't go without permission now that I'm a guardian. It's the rules we have to go by now, Pibby!"

"You do what you want to. I'm going now!" I shouted as I jumped in Pesco's open mouth.

"I can't, I'm sorry!" Squeaky said.

"Suit yourself!" Pesco closed his mouth and disappeared underwater. I was steaming mad that Squeaky refused to go.

CHAPTER 21

Next Adventure

I shouted out loud so Pesco could hear me from inside, "Take me as close as you can get to Sova's forest!" I knew I couldn't do it alone. I had to find help.

After a few hours, Pesco stopped at the bank inside Sova's forest. Pesco opened his mouth and let me out. "Do you have any more friends that you can bring here?" I asked.

"Sure!" Pesco answered. "I will have them here in a day's time! Meet me right here tomorrow at this time!"

"Okay, thanks, Pesco!" I took off toward the place in the forest where I hoped I'd find Sova. It was the same place I found him the last two times, so I was hoping he'd be there. I arrived at the tree that Sova sat in when I stabbed him and made him fall and break his wing. When I got there, there was no sign of Sova. I decided I'd wait in the hole Squeaky and I hid in from Sova. I drifted off to sleep while waiting on him to show.

"Well! You never know who might show up at your door step," Sova said, waking me up. "What do I owe this honor to? The guardian of the grove came visiting so soon? I'm honored," Sova boosted.

"There's trouble at the waterfall. Mr. Lapin, Mr. Mudar, and several animals were taken by Shonta's snakes and what's left of the crew we defeated at the cliffs," I answered.

"That means they probably have Tonito's crew also," Sova said.

119

"We should've finished them while we had the chance! We can't do this alone. Sova, do you have any other like you that would help?"

"I'm not sure they wouldn't be worse than the enemy you're fighting. You know they hunt animals like you, Pibby," Sova said.

"Just tell them they can eat any of our enemies they would like. Just make sure they know the difference." I chuckled.

"Stay here. I'll fly over to their territories to talk to them. I'm not promising you anything though. These guys are meaner than I was," Sova answered.

I went back in the hole as Sova flew off toward the others territories. I still couldn't believe Squeaky wasn't with me.

Meanwhile, Squeaky went back to the guardians to ask for permission to join me.

"We can't interfere if it doesn't concern the grove," the guardians said.

"These animals saved the grove just yesterday! Now you won't help them!" Squeaky shouted.

"We can't risk losing more animals to some senseless battle. We lost too many at the cliffs. You must follow our rules as a guardian!"

Solace came out of the hole home and asked Squeaky where I was. Squeaky told her where I was and what I was planning.

"You must help, Father! Pibby risked his life to save me and bring me home!"

"The decision has been made. The guardians will only defend the grove!" her dad answered.

Solace stormed back into her home, crying. Squeaky knew if he left the grove, he would be losing something he wanted since he was a boy.

"Get back to your duties, Squeaky!" his dad shouted. Squeaky walked off toward the grove to return to his duties. He was torn up inside for failing me. *What if something happens to Pibby? I'll never forgive myself. What should I do?* Squeaky was asking himself.

*****

Back at Sova's forest, I was still waiting for Sova to return. He knew I had to meet Pesco back at the stream the next day, so Sova had to return before then. *I have to come up with a plan before I get back to Pesco*, I thought to myself.

I fell asleep waiting and thinking about what to do. Early the next morning, I heard someone talking outside the hole and poked my head out to see Sova and four others like him.

"Meet my brothers!" Sova said. "They agreed to help as long as they get to keep all the leftovers, if you know what I mean?"

"Fine with me!" I said. "Tell them to get a good look at me. I'm not a leftover!" They all laughed at me. "Okay, we got to fly to the stream to meet Pesco. He's supposed to bring some friends to help. They also are not leftovers!"

"I've got this vest Mr. Lapin made. Put it on, and I'll grab you," Sova said. I put the vest on, and Sova grabbed me in flight, and we were off toward the stream.

My and his newly made friends arrived at the stream to find Pesco and a few of his friends waiting. The three beavers dived back in the water when they saw Sova and his brothers fly up. The two gators hissed and opened their mouths to defend themselves.

Pesco shouted, "Any friend of Pibby is a friend of ours!" All the animals, including two more fish like Pesco, came back to the bank. "This is all I could round up in such short notice, Pibby!"

"This is fine!" I shouted. "I thank all of you for coming to help. I'm afraid we're gonna be outnumbered by a good bit. We've got to try though."

I looked at one of the gators and asked, "Aren't you the one who tried to eat us on the boat?"

"So sorry, young squirrel, we've got to eat just like you! Jacare is the name!" the gator answered.

"Well, Jacare, if y'all get hungry, don't eat the good guys, okay?"

"Deal, my young friend!" Jacare said.

Pesco introduced the beavers as the Bobor brothers. "They don't talk much, but they are good listeners. These two girls like me are Riba and Kala. They are my sisters."

"Well, this is Sova and his brothers, and they also promised not to eat the good guys!" I shouted. "We think they have all our friends at the waterfall lake. I'm sure they have it guarded well with the hawks in the air. Sova, do you think y'all can fly close and see what we're up against?" I asked.

"If we fly together as a group, they won't dare attack us! We'll just fly over as if we're just flying through, not to raise any suspicions," Sova answered.

"Pesco, can the Bobor brothers dam the stream just above the falls begin? We'll flood the whole valley pushing them up in the forest," I said.

One of the Bobor brothers spoke up and said, "It'll take days for it to flood the whole valley!"

"That's okay!" I said. "It'll sneak up on them slowly. Plus, you know how much cats hate water! It'll divide their forces up!"

"We head upstream and start that dam. Give us a day or two to get it built though," the Bobor brothers said as they swam off.

"Jacare, when the waters get high enough, you and your brothers swim in and put yourselves in position to take out whoever is leading them," I said. "Pesco, if the waters get high enough, y'all can help take some of the snakes out. If we can free enough of them, we'll have ourselves a little army. If not, don't risk your lives for me. Get back to the stream and go back home!"

Sova spoke up and said, "We can't handle a lot of hawks at one time."

"Maybe you won't have to. Mr. Lapin has built many weapons at his place. If we can free enough animals, we'll have bows like before at the cliffs," I answered. "If not, just lead them away from the battle as long as you can."

Sova agreed and he and his brothers flew away to investigate the falls area.

I said, "We've got some time before they get the dam built, so get some rest and food," pointing at the gators.

They all laughed and sunk back down in the water. I sat on the limb, hoping my plan was a good one. I knew we were outnumbered and the odds were against him. These animals helped me rescue Solace, so I was gonna try to help them. *I wish I had Squeaky here to help though*, I thought to myself.

*****

PIBBY'S ADVENTURES

Squeaky made his rounds like he was told to by his dad, but he couldn't get me off his mind. Solace was waiting on him at his hole home when he got there.

"Why aren't you with Pibby?" she shouted. "He stood by you and actually saved your life a couple of times!"

"I'll lose my spot as a guardian and the respect of my dad. Do you know how long it took to get him to notice that I was actually alive?" Squeaky answered.

"Well, I think you're gonna regret this till the day you die!" she shouted as she stormed away.

*****

Solace tossed and turned all night, worrying about me. Suddenly, she got an idea. "If I go to Pibby, my dad will send Squeaky to get me. I'm leaving first thing in the morning!" she said to herself.

Solace was packed and ready before the sun came up. She knew this was probably not the smartest move in the world, but she had to help me in any way she could.

Soon as daylight showed itself, Solace was on the move toward the waterfall. She knew they wouldn't miss her till she didn't show up tonight. That would give her a whole day start on them. Hopefully, she'd be out of the grove by then.

By the time Squeaky started his rounds, Solace was halfway across the grove. Squeaky thought he would visit Mr. Mudar today to see how he was getting along. He normally wouldn't visit him during his rounds, but he needed to talk to someone. The guilt was killing him, and he needed some reassurance that he was doing the right thing.

As he got closer, he noticed Mr. Mudar's place was kinda in a mess on the outside. *This isn't like him. He's usually the neatest animal in the grove*, Squeaky thought as he knocked on Mudar's door.

There was no answer after knocking three times. He tried opening the door but to no avail. Maybe he was visiting or just rambling about. *I'll try to be back later on in the day.* Squeaky got back to his rounds, checking on the borders of the grove.

*****

Solace was making good time as she entered the last head of woods inside the grove. She was determined to make it outside the grove before dark. The woods started getting dark as the evening faded. Solace picked up her pace. She knew she didn't want to be in here after dark.

*****

Squeaky was finishing up his rounds when he came back to Mr. Mudar's place. There was still nobody around, and everything was dark. Something was wrong, and Squeaky knew it. He decided to break in and look for himself. After prying the door open, he noticed no one had been here in a while. Squeaky quickly left Mudar's place to notify his dad. It was dark when Squeaky reached home to tell his dad.

"Mr. Mudar is missing. I just left his house, and he hasn't been there in days," Squeaky said.

Just as he was finished saying this, Solace's father walked up behind him and asked, "Is Solace with you?"

"No, sir," Squeaky answered.

"She hasn't been home all day, and no one has seen her."

"Squeaky was just telling me Mr. Mudar is gone also. You don't reckon she went to help Pibby?" Squeaky's dad asked.

"Well, Squeaky, here is your chance. Go bring her back. Don't let her get out of this grove! You're gonna have to travel in the dark to find her, so get at it!" his dad shouted. "And don't leave this grove!"

"Yes, sir!" Squeaky answered, running out the door.

*****

Solace made it to the edge of the grove and settled in a hole for the night.

CHAPTER 22

Squeaky's Dilemma

Squeaky ran most of the way for the first hour but slowed a bit as it was totally dark now. He knew the place like the back of his hand, so the dark didn't bother him. What did bother him was that Solace was out here by herself. He knew she was headed toward the falls, so he was on the right path. Solace wasn't gonna travel at night, so he knew he was gaining on her as she slept in a tree somewhere.

*****

Solace was fast asleep in a warm hole in an old cypress tree on the edge of the grove. She would slow down tomorrow to see if the guardian did as she expected. If they did, Squeaky would be there soon. Then maybe she could talk some sense into him.

*****

Squeaky traveled all night and came to the edge of the grove couple hours before daylight. He began shouting Solace's name, not figuring that she made it much farther than he had already. Squeaky stopped and settled in a hole till dawn arrived. The sun rose on a foggy day on the edge of the grove.

*****

Solace started down the old cypress tree that kept her warm through the night. About the time she reached the bottom of the tree, she heard Squeaky shouting her name. "Over here!" she shouted back.

Squeaky ran over to her, hugging her. "Are you crazy? What are you doing out here all alone? Your dad told me to bring you home," Squeaky said.

"I'm going to help Pibby, like you should be! He's your friend, Squeaky! We're halfway there, come on!" Solace screamed. "We'll tell Dad it took a long time to find me."

Squeaky just walked in circles, thinking. "I don't know. I don't know."

"What would he do if he were in your shoes?" she asked.

The minute she asked, he knew what I would do. "Okay!" Squeaky said.

"You must be careful though! Let's go!" she said. "Pibby may be in trouble!"

They headed down the trail toward the falls. Squeaky felt better after his decision to go. He knew all along it was the right thing to do. It would be two days before they would reach the falls, not knowing what they'd find.

*****

I waited for Sova to return with information. Meanwhile, the beavers were working on the dam as planned. It would take a while to dam the whole stream, but it could be done. They were taking down tree by tree along the bank to build it. After they complete the dam, it would slowly flood the falls area, forcing all the animals toward the forest.

The cat crew had taken control of the emperor's animals and helping them to get back the princess. The hawks joined them to help get another chance to capture me. The emperor's animals thought Solace was some kinda queen because of her blue eyes. They'd never saw a squirrel with blue eyes, so she had to be someone that means something to their future. In their eyes, they were rescuing her to protect her. They convinced the cat crew and the hawks of the same thing. Shonta's snake crew just wanted revenge for Shonta's death.

Together, they made a pretty formidable force to deal with. That was if they didn't kill each other before they got the princess back. The lead cat name was Kocka. He was the oldest of the whole crew. His plan was to wait on me to come and rescue his friends. At that time, he would either take the princess or trade her for his prisoners.

Kocka had his crew build a round cell out of rocks with logs across the top to keep his prisoners in. Mr. Mudar and Mr. Lapin along with several from the grove were in the cell.

Mr. Lapin was trying to calm all the animals down in the cell. "It'll be okay, everyone! I don't think their plan is to hurt us. If it was, we'd be already dead."

"They're waiting on Pibby to show up, I think," Mr. Mudar added.

A lot of the animals from the falls were in the cell also.

"Why do they want the princess so bad?" everyone asked.

"She's special. She doesn't even know how special she is," Mr. Mudar said. "She's the key to all of us continuing to be able to communicate like we do. As long as we have a blue-eyed animal in our midst, we can hear and talk to each other like we do. It can only happen when a changer and an animal have a baby together, like her mother and the black guardian. If something happens to her, we all start acting like real animals again, killing and eating each other. One of her offspring will be blue-eyed. That's why they guard her so closely."

"That makes no sense!" They all laughed.

Mr. Mudar laughed with them, but he knew he was right because he remembered the last blue-eyed animal. It was his daughter that disappeared one day. Solace's mother appeared the same day his daughter disappeared. He knew there was a connection but just couldn't figure it out. That would have to wait. They gotta get out of this mess first.

Mr. Mudar noticed the floor of the cell seem to be soggier than it was before. He didn't think much about at the time.

*****

I saw Sova and his brothers off in the distant headed my way. I was anxious to see what they figured out. Sova landed first, his brothers right behind him.

"We've got problems, Pibby! They've got the whole place covered in cats, snakes, and hawks. Looks like they've built a cell to keep all the prisoners in," Sova said.

"We'll flood them out, then move in, and save the animals. Once they're safe, we'll figure out how to handle the rest," I said.

"The beavers are about a half a day from the dam being done. It'll take two days to flood them out, so we need to fill Pesco in on the plan," Sova said.

I walked over to the bank, grabbed a limb, and hit the water three times. That'd bring him shortly.

*****

Squeaky was leading the way through the forest when Solace shouted, "Stop!"

"What is it?" Squeaky asked.

"Hawks flying above!"

They both ran under a log and hid.

"We must be getting close. You think they have Pibby?" Solace asked.

"We need to get closer to see what's going on."

They kept undercover as they moved toward the falls. Squeaky led the way to this huge bush. They crawled up in it and sat and watched. They could see the cats all gathered up near the falls but noticed the snakes anywhere.

"That building by the falls wasn't there before," Solace whispered. "That's probably where Mr. Mudar and the others are. Why are they doing this?" she asked.

Squeaky didn't want to say, but she had to know eventually. "It's because they want you back in the city. You're the key to all of us. As long as you're here, we can live like we do. We live almost like humans do now. It's because of you, or at least that's what everyone thinks. As long as there is a half-breed blue-eyed animal in our midst, we can have this kind of life. They want to take you to the city and lock you up somewhere that no one can get to you. Why do you think the emperor wanted to marry you? He wanted his offspring to be special like you," Squeaky said.

Solace stared at him like he was crazy. "Have you lost your mind? That is the stupidest thing I've ever heard in my life!" Solace chuckled.

"I know, but it's true. There was a time when we couldn't talk or build things like humans do, but since animals like you started showing up, it all changed. That's why your dad is so protective over you."

Solace just kept staring at him and said, "So I am a princess?"

"In a kinda sorta way," Squeaky said, rolling his eyes.

"Well, a lady could get used to that!" she said.

Squeaky thought to himself, *I've probably just created a monster.*

They stayed in the bush for the rest of the day, watching the cats at the falls. The snakes never showed themselves, making them wonder what they were up to. Squeaky noticed the water level had come up during the day. It was almost to the cell now.

"Oh well," he said. "It probably rained upstream last night. Let's go back to the hole for the night and come back tomorrow."

"You have my permission!" Solace giggled.

Squeaky rolled his eyes and headed back to the tree where they stayed in last night.

*****

Pesco popped his head up right in front of me, startling me. "What's up, Pibby?"

"Pesco, do you think the water will rise enough for you and your sisters to ease into their camp?" I asked.

"Not sure, but we'll give it a try tomorrow night. Do you want us to carry you in?"

"That's what I was thinking," I answered. "Sova, your job is to get the hawks' attention while I rescue Mr. Mudar and the others. Maybe we'll push them back to the forest where we'll have the trees for protection. That leaves Shonta's snakes. How do we handle them?" I asked.

Pesco spoke up, "If they stay in the water and we can get in there, we can pull them under till they get scared off."

"That's a big *if*," I said.

"We've gotta try, and that's all I can come up with."

I had doubts his plan would work, but it's all we had. "Let's meet right here tomorrow evening, and we'll get after them."

They all said okay and left. I crawled up the tree and watched the stream continue to rise.

CHAPTER 23

Battle at the Falls

The next day, Kocka noticed the water rising and told everyone to back toward the forest a little.

"What about the prisoners?" one of the guards asked.

"Leave them in there. Maybe it'll let them know we're serious. Something tells me we'll see the heroes soon."

The cat crew moved back toward the forest with their camp. In the water around the falls were snakes with their whole body cooling in the water. The hawks were perched in the trees at the edge of the forest. Mr. Mudar and the rest were up to their knees in water.

Mr. Lapin said, "I've never seen the water rise like this here."

Mr. Mudar asked, "Never?"

"No, sir, and I've lived here for a long time!"

Mr. Mudar laughed and said, "Smart squirrel that Pibby is. He's doing this to get their attention and spread them out toward the forest."

*****

Jacare and his crew had swum in early that morning to get a closer look. They noticed all the cats were a good ways from the cell now. They headed back to me to tell me what they saw. Meanwhile, Squeaky and Solace were back in the bush watching the water rise.

"It won't be long now!" Squeaky said.

"How do you know? Won't be long for what?"

"Pibby has a plan, and the rising stream is part of it. I have to find a way to get over there through all that water. I need to be up high so I can protect him with my bow."

"Let's just ride a limb over to that one tree by the falls. They'll never see us," Solace said.

"Us? You're staying right here!" Squeaky demanded. "Did you not listen to one thing I said yesterday?"

"Okay, okay!" she said.

Squeaky found a limb that was a little bigger than he was and took it to the edge of the water. He climbed on and lay down so he could paddle his way over. Solace prayed that one of the hawks wouldn't see him. Squeaky moved so slow that he didn't make a ripple. It took him nearly an hour to make it to the bottom of the tree.

After slowly climbing as high as he could while still staying camouflaged, he settled in waiting for me. Squeaky noticed there were about ten snakes in the water. That was the reason he couldn't see them before. He could see down in the cell where about twenty animals were held. The water was still rising, almost up to their chests now.

Looking toward the stream, he could see three large fish headed to the falls. "Pesco!" he said to himself. "It's about to go down!"

About that time, Sova and his brothers flew down and each grabbed a snake and flew as high as they could before dropping them on the boulders in the field. The other snakes dove underwater for cover. Immediately, the hawks left the trees and headed for the falls. Sova and his brothers cut them off, and they tied up with three of them.

As they were fighting by the edge of the forest, Pesco swam up beside the cell and let me out. I waded to the door and unlocked it. Mr. Mudar and the others all jumped in Pesco's and his sisters' mouths.

"Pesco! Take them to safety!" I shouted. "I'll keep the snakes busy while you head back to the stream."

About the time Pesco and his sisters sunk underwater, the snakes reappeared in the falls. One came right at me with his mouth open and fangs dripping with venom. I jumped up to the top of the

PIBBY'S ADVENTURES

cell and down in it. The water was almost at his neck, but the snake couldn't get in yet. The door was too small for the snakes to enter.

I knew this wouldn't save me once the water rose to where we could come over the top. One snake finally stuck his head over the top, and Squeaky drove an arrow right between his eyes. I looked up in the tree to see Squeaky perched in a shooter's position. By then, Sova was leading the hawks away from the falls. They had taken down two or three of them, but there was too many to face at one time.

Meanwhile, the cats couldn't do anything 'cause the water was to the edge of the forest by now. The snakes were hiding behind the falls after Squeaky nailed the first one. Squeaky motioned for me to come to him. He didn't wanna give his position away to the snakes. I climbed out and swam to the base of the tree and up to Squeaky I went.

About that time, the beavers poked their heads out of the water and shouted, "The dam is gonna blow! It can't take much more!"

I knew the cats would be on top of them as soon as the water went down. Every time a snake would peek around the corner, Squeaky would bury an arrow in their heads. Suddenly, we heard a loud crashing noise, and the water was rushing by us so hard that it took the tree we were in with. We both went crashing in the water and trapped in the current headed to the stream.

I looked back and saw two of the snakes right behind us. I went down under till the first snake was over me and came up with my sword through the bottom of my mouth. The second one was about to grab Squeaky and suddenly disappeared under the water. The current carried me and Squeaky way downstream before we managed to reach the bank and get out.

Meanwhile, Kocka's cat crew were all over the falls, looking for me. "Spread out, they can't be far from here!" he shouted.

*****

There were only three snakes left in Shonta's crew, and they were just getting back to the falls. The hawks gave up on catching Sova

133

and his brothers and were almost back at the falls. Once the hawks returned, Kocka told them to search downstream for the so-called heroes. The snakes were already in the stream looking by now.

*****

Squeaky and I were exhausted from trying not to drown. They could barely stand up and catch a breath. The snakes arrived about the time the hawks did. All Squeaky and I could do was to surrender. The hawks grabbed us by our clothes and flew us back to Kocka at the falls.

The hawks dropped us through the top of the cell to the ground. Then all the hawks perched themselves on the walls of the cell.

"Well, that was a nice trade!" Kocka laughed. "A few unknown animals for the heroes of the grove! Surely the princess will come for the love of her life!"

*****

Solace watched it all, crying from the bush she was hiding in. She didn't know what to do. The sun was almost down as she crawled back to the hole.

*****

Pesco went back to where he left all the animals he saved. He poked his head up and told them what had happened. Sova said, "We'll go get them!"

"Pesco said, "You can't. All the hawks are guarding them now. The snakes and cats would get to them before you could."

Mr. Mudar said, "It's getting dark. Let's all find places to stay near. We'll meet here in the morning and figure it out."

They all found trees to stay in for the night. Mr. Lapin found a hole right next to the ground he and Mr. Mudar could fit into. When they got settled in the hole, Mudar said, "You know we can't give up the princess for them."

Lapin replied, "I know, and they know that also."

CHAPTER 24

The Trade

I was exhausted along with Squeaky. We had been lying in the cell for hours without water or any kinda food. We didn't have the strength to move, much less try to escape.

Kocka, the cat leader, came to the door and made the guard get Squeaky up. "Bring him to me!" he demanded.

The guard went in and grabbed Squeaky and dragged him outside to Kocka.

"I want you to go to your guardians and tell them that their heroes get no food nor water till I receive the princess. From the looks of him, he won't last long, so I suggest you make her show soon! Now get going, squirrel!" Kocka shouted.

Squeaky, barely being able to walk, headed out of their camp toward the forest. He knew it wouldn't be long until I would need water.

Back at the stream's edge, the animals had gathered back together, discussing what to do. Jacare the gator had just returned and told them about Kocka releasing Squeaky and his deal proposal.

Sova said, "I'll go pick up Squeaky once he hits the forest's edge and bring him back here." Sova flew off and headed around the camp so they couldn't spot him.

Mr. Mudar said, "The guardians will never trade the princess for anyone! We're gonna have to save him ourselves."

"That's impossible!" they all said at once.

KEITH MOCK

"The cats and hawks are standing guard, close this time," Jacare said.

"We'll figure something out, and it's gotta be soon."

*****

Sova flew around to the edge of the woods and watched Squeaky drag himself across the open field. As Squeaky entered the forest, Sova flew down to him. "What kinda shape you in, buddy?" Sova asked.

"I'm just tired. I'll be fine once I get some rest. Pibby is gonna be in trouble shortly if he doesn't get any water," Squeaky answered.

"In trouble! What do you mean?" Solace asked, walking up from behind them.

Sova shouted, "What is she doing here?"

"She convinced me to come help Pibby save the other animals. That didn't turn out to be good for Pibby though," Squeaky answered.

"What's wrong with Pibby?" Solace shouted again.

"He's in the cell without any water or food till they get you. He won't last long either. All the others are on the bank at the stream."

"Let me take Squeaky over to meet them, and, Solace, you go home," Sova demanded.

"It's too risky to let her go by herself. We can protect her better if she's with us," Squeaky said.

"You couldn't make her go home anyway!"

"Take us over, Sova!"

Sova grabbed both of them and flew back around the camp to the bank where everyone was. Mr. Mudar was the first to greet Solace, exclaiming how she shouldn't be here. Solace just gave him a stern look and walked away.

Tonito sat with his arms crossed and asked Mr. Lapin where he stored all his bows he had made. Mr. Lapin told them they were stored in his shop at the back of the camp. "You think you could lead us to through these woods without being seen?" Tonito asked.

PIBBY'S ADVENTURES

"Sure, it's covered pretty well, but we'll have to be quiet. I've made enough for everyone here. I get carried away when I'm in my shop sometimes," Lapin replied.

"We'll take my crew and get the bows while y'all figure out something. You know we're gonna need weapons," Tonito said.

"Okay, but be careful. We're gonna need everyone on this one," Squeaky said. "We're gonna have to hit them when they don't expect us to."

"I think at night is the best idea. They'll be sleeping. I can fly in and grab him and be gone!" Sova said.

"There's no way you can swoop down in that cell. It's way too small for you. We need to sneak in and dig him out from the back side of the cell," Squeaky said.

"That'll take a long time, and we'll never do that without alerting them!"

"Ticker!" Solace shouted. "The mole at the hawks' gorge! He could dig his way under the cell and Pibby could follow him out, like we did at the gorge."

"That's a pretty long way to the gorge, and Pibby doesn't have very long," Squeaky said.

"I fly Solace to the gorge and find this Ticker and bring him back," Sova said. "Come on, we've got to get going! And don't worry, I'll protect her with my life. After all, she saved mine not too long ago."

"Let's go!" Solace said.

Before anyone could argue about it, Sova and Solace were flying off. Tonito and his crew were headed to Mr. Lapin's shop for the weapons. Mr. Mudar and Squeaky were drawing plans on the ground in front of the rest.

*****

At the cell, I had sat up and felt a little better. I was feeling my need for water, and it started to take effect a little. In my mind, I wondered what kinda rescue plan Squeaky was planning. I knew the guardians wouldn't give up Solace, and I didn't want them to. I didn't know about Solace's importance to all the animals, but she was special to me in another way. I couldn't see my life without her in it. I intended to tell her that if I made it out here alive.

I could hear Kocka talking outside the cell. "Once we get the princess, we'll go the grove and get rid of all the animals there and cure them ever trying to rescue her again. We'll let this one rot in the cell and make sure we get the bow and arrow dude."

I heard them coming, so I decided to act like I was worse off than I actually was. I lay on my belly in the middle of the cell, pretending to be passed out.

The guard looked in and said to Kocka, "Don't think we're gonna have to worry about this one much longer!"

I noticed that they didn't even take my sword before they dropped me in the cell. Lying there, I decided I would conserve my energy till Squeaky would do what he was gonna do.

*****

Squeaky was drawing out in the dirt how they were gonna distract the cats and hawks while Ticker hopefully digs me out.

"We'll come from the front of the falls and see if we can draw most of them to us. I know they'll leave some to guard with Pibby, but at least it'll spread them out. We'll post Tonito's crew in the edge of the forest in the trees. Jacare and his brothers can handle the three last remaining snakes. Sova can try to fight the hawks off."

Meanwhile, Sova and Solace were almost to the gorge where she last saw Ticker. Sova landed on the cliff above the gorge and let Solace down. Solace started calling Ticker's name out loud. She went over to where the old tunnel was that led to Ticker's home.

"I'm gonna crawl down this tunnel to see if I can find him."

"Okay. I'll stand guard out here, be careful!" Sova shouted.

Solace started down the hole headfirst. She had forgotten how tight of a fit it was. She squeezed her way to the room where they spent the night. Solace noticed Ticker standing in the corner, shaking like a leaf. Ticker pointed to the other side of the room at a snake curling up asleep with its head pointed toward them.

PIBBY'S ADVENTURES

Solace almost screamed but held it in barely. Ticker motioned for her to go back up the tunnel, and he was gonna make his on tunnel to escape in. Solace knew Ticker wouldn't be fast enough to escape the snake, having to dig his way out.

She waited for Ticker to start digging, and as the snake woke up, she screamed, "Over here!" and took off up the tunnel. The snake immediately came across the room and up the tunnel after her. Solace climbed for her life. She could feel the snake touching her feet.

As she came out of the tunnel, she jumped to her feet, then fell on her back. The snake came flying out the hole with its mouth open on top of her. Sova grabbed the snake's head with his claws and drove them through his head. Solace screamed as loud as she could and fainted.

About that time, Tinker come barreling from underground, standing beside her, protecting her from Sova.

"Hold on, little fellow! I'm a friend," Sova said.

Ticker kept growling at him till Solace woke up and said, "It's okay, he's with me."

Ticker calmed down and asked what they were doing here. Solace explained why they came to get him, and he graciously accepted.

"You just saved me from getting eaten by a snake. How can I refuse you?" Ticker said.

Sova grabbed both of them and headed back to the others.

*****

Tonito's crew were following Mr. Lapin through the woods to his shop. They were careful not to make any noise once they reached the shop. The shop was an old barn type with tables full of things Mr. Lapin had made.

"Lot of time on your hands, I see, Lapin?" Tonito whispered.

Lapin smiled and pointed to the table with all the bows on it. He directed a few of the crew to all the arrows he had made in the corner of the shop. They could hear the cats talking off in the distance. Tonito had left two outside to keep watch.

The crew gathered all the bows and arrows and made their way to the trees behind the shop. After an hour or two, they were back at the bank of the stream with the others.

Squeaky said, "Good job," and grabbed one of the bows and gave it a try. "Let's all make our way through the woods to the front of the lake. Pesco, when Sova returns, tell him the rest of our plan."

"When I see Sova fly over the camp, I'll know when to attack," Pesco said. "Okay, if anyone gets in trouble, come back to the bank, and I'll take them to safety. I'll have Solace with me the whole time."

"Okay, good luck!" Squeaky said as he was leaving.

They made their long way around the camp to the front of the falls. Squeaky told Tonito to put his guys in all the trees on the edge of the forest. Jacare and his gator brothers were already headed across the field to sneak in the lake at the falls. Squeaky joined Tonito's crew in the trees. All he was waiting for was Sova's sign.

Sova and his passengers arrived at the stream greeted by Pesco. He explained what Squeaky had planned and told Solace she was to stay with him. Sova told Ticker he would drop him as close as he could to the cell, but the rest was up to him. Ticker shook his head okay.

Sova looked at Pesco and said, "Keep her safe!"

"You don't have to worry about her. She's in a good mouth," he said, smiling. "They'll have to go deep to find her."

"Good luck, Ticker, please bring Pibby back!" Solace said, climbing in Pesco's mouth.

Sova picked Ticker up and headed toward the camp with his two sisters beside him. Sova's two sisters reached the camp first and drew the attention of the camp while Sova dropped Ticker by Mr. Lapin's shop.

"That's the cell over there," Sova told Ticker. Sova flew over the camp with a loud screech, and the whole camp heard. The hawks took off after Sova and his sisters across the field.

Kocka shouted, "Keep some guards on the prisoner! They'll be trying to bust him out!"

The guard looked in at me, who was still lying face down in the dirt. I was wide awake and ready to do whatever it took to escape.

*****

PIBBY'S ADVENTURES

Ticker had made his way to the side of the cell and already started tunneling his way in. Jacare and his gator brothers were right behind the three snakes as they turned to get out of the lake. It took a minute to rid every one of the snakes. After taking care of the snakes, they turned their sights to the cats, just waiting for one to venture too close to the lake's edge.

As Sova made it to the forest's edge, the hawks were not far behind. The first hawk went down, courtesy of Squeaky's arrow. Then the hawks met a barrage of arrows as they passed overhead. The hawks were dropping like flies.

*****

Ticker surfaced right beside me. "Ticker!" I whispered.

"Let's go. We don't have much time!" Ticker whispered back.

I followed Ticker back through the tunnel to the outside of the cell.

"This way," Ticker said. "We're meeting this big fish at the stream!"

We ran through the woods as fast as Ticker's little feet could go.

*****

The last hawk fell at the expense of Tonito's arrow. Squeaky shouted, "Everyone, make their way back to the stream!"

They all went back the way they came, being protected from the sky by Sova and his sisters. After seeing the last hawk fall, Kocka called all his cat crew to guard the cell. "No one gets near the cell! Guard it with your life!"

"There's nothing to guard!" one of the guards shouted.

Kocka ran over to the door and looked in at the hole in the ground. "I've had it with these cotton-picking animals! Pack it up! We're going to the grove to settle this once and for all!"

*****

Sova and the crew made it back around to the bank where everyone was celebrating and hugging one another. Squeaky walked up to me. I grabbed him, hugged him, and said, "Good job, brother!"

Pesco popped his head up, and Solace jumped out of his mouth and ran to me and landed a huge kiss on my lips. Everyone looked at us and started clapping.

Sova held Ticker as high as he could and said, "Here's your hero!"

Ticker was taking it all in, bowing his head down to the crowd of animals applauding for him.

Mr. Mudar shook his head and said, "I never would have believed we could have done it."

Jacare and his gator brothers arrived at the bank during all the celebration and shouted, "We got more problems! The cat crew are headed to the grove to wipe everyone out. We heard their leader say it before we left."

We all took off through the forest toward the grove. Silence covered the group of animals instantly. They all turned to me, as to ask, "What do we do now?"

I sat in silence for a few minutes and finally said, "Sova, you and your sisters will fly six of us with bows to get ahead of the cats. The rest of you will catch up from behind. We'll have them trapped between us. Pesco, take Ticker and Solace up the creek to the grove. Solace, he'll get you close as he can to your father's place. You must warn them of the danger that's coming their way. Then they can warn the grove's animals."

CHAPTER 25

The Grove's Fate

"Jacare, you and your gator buddies follow Pesco upstream to protect Solace on her way home."

Sova grabbed me and Squeaky and headed out to get in front of the cats. Sova's brothers grabbed Tonito and some of his crew and followed Sova. Pesco and his sisters left with mouthfuls of animals headed to the grove. The rest of Tonito's crew and animals from the falls started to follow behind where the cats entered the forest.

Kocka's cat crew were moving fast through the forest toward the grove. Kocka's numbers were about forty cats, no more hawks or snakes. Kocka knew he could wreak havoc on the grove with that many cats. He figured to get rid of the grove and he could rule it all and have the princess. Kocka figured he would take the princess back to the city and build a place to keep her hidden and safe. He knew that she held the key to being able to live the way they do. The princess had to be kept safe.

The cats spread out over a big area and walked in unison toward the grove. It would take a day or two to reach the edge of the grove.

Sova flew over the cat crew below and kept going so I could actually have time to set something up for Kocka as they come through. I didn't know how I was gonna stop forty cats from doing anything they want, but I sure wasn't giving up now. I had to figure a way to at least slow them down so Solace could warn the grove.

I suddenly got an idea. I shouted for Sova to turn to the left and fly toward my grandfather's house. Sova did as told, and his sisters followed.

*****

Pesco was making good time swimming upstream toward the grove. He would arrive a lot sooner than the rest 'cause the stream was a straight shot by the grove. Mr. Mudar was with Solace and Mr. Lapin. They had discussed what each one would do when they reach the grove. Solace would head to the guardians and inform them of the danger coming. Mudar and Lapin would spread out and warn the grove animals.

*****

Squeaky and I could see my granddaddy's farm up ahead. Sova dropped us down right by the Mr. Pibb can I named myself after. Squeaky looked down at it and laughed at me. I told Sova and his sisters to wait here till Squeaky and I returned.

Meanwhile, Tonito and his crew crawled up to the tree and waited also.

"Follow me, Squeaky, we're going to that barn in the back!" I shouted. I ran across the yard toward the barn with Squeaky in tow. No one was around in the middle of the day, so it was easy to make it across the yard. We made it to the barn and climbed up in the loft.

Squeaky asked, "What are we doing here?"

I walked over to the cages in the back and shouted, "Wake up, guys!"

"Who in the world is waking us up in the middle of the day?" a big blue-ticked deer dog said in the pen.

The other ten dogs started complaining as I shouted, "Up here, boys!"

"What do you want, little man?" the oldest dog said.

"I used to be one of the little boys that lived on this farm. I need y'all help really bad!"

PIBBY'S ADVENTURES

"I think you ate some bad acorns, little man. Say you used to be a boy, huh? Anyway, what kind of help do you need?"

"We've got forty cats headed to the grove to take over," I said.

"Only the city has that many cats!" the dogs barked.

"That's where they're coming from. If they take over, all the animals around here will leave, including the deer."

That got the dogs' attention. They all stood up and started shouting at each other.

"I'll open the cage if y'all agree to follow us and wait for the cats to arrive in the grove!" I shouted.

"So let me get this right. You'll let us out, and we get to chase cats?" the old dog asked.

"Exactly right!" I answered.

They all started shouting, "I'm in!"

"Okay, let me see if I can get the door open. When I do, let's meet at that tree over there!" I said, pointing at the tree.

Squeaky and I crawled down to the lock on the door and unlatched it. The door swung open, and all ten dogs rushed out shouting. Squeaky and I headed back to the tree and crawled up passed the dogs.

"Okay, follow us as we fly toward the area we'll set up!" Sova grabbed us again and took off with his sisters following. The dogs followed below and loved every minute of it.

Back at the stream bank, Pesco was letting all his passengers out and his friends doing the same. Solace waited for Jacare and his gator friends to climb out before she headed to her home. The gators followed close behind, not letting her out of their sight.

Mr. Mudar and Mr. Lapin headed their separate ways to warn the animals in the grove.

*****

It didn't take long for me to reach my ambush spot I picked out. I asked the dogs to split up five on one side, five on the other. The five others that came with me and I would wait in the middle for Kocka. Sova and his brothers would fly back behind the cats and help the animals bringing up the rear.

My friends and I were all in place and waiting. Meanwhile, Solace reached her dad, and after receiving a firm talk about her disappearance, she explained the danger headed this way. Her dad made her stay in the house, and he and the two other guardians grabbed their weapons and headed out to meet me.

The cats were about an hour from my position and were moving fast. Kocka was leading the way, keeping the cats spread out. The crew behind the cats were closing in on Kocka's crew. Everyone in their group were armed with bows. There were many different animals in this group from the falls.

Solace waited till her dad left and followed him from a distance. There was no way she wasn't gonna be there for me. She figured that if they lost, it was over anyway.

The guardians reached me and asked where I wanted them to be. I asked them to stand together in the open to draw Kocka to the right spot. They gladly agreed to and moved into place.

Solace climbed a tree behind all of us to watch over me. Kocka showed up right in front of the guardians and stopped.

"What is this? A welcoming committee!" Kocka shouted. "Look, boys, they sent their guardians to stop us!" All the cats moved up behind Kocka and were laughing at the fox squirrels with bows pointed at them.

I stepped out along with Squeaky and the others. "Whoa, now we have nine whole squirrels to eat, boys!" Kocka laughed.

About that time, all the animals with Sova and his brothers showed up behind them.

"You could have two hundred animals, and we would still win, and you know it! So give up and give us the princess, and we'll let you live!" Kocka demanded.

"We have ten more friends I want you to meet!" I shouted as I whistled out loud.

The dogs came up on both sides of the cats with snarling teeth showing. The old dog shouted, "Look, boys, we have forty whole cats to eat!" The dogs moved in closer.

Kocka shouted, "Okay, okay, we'll leave and go back to the city."

PIBBY'S ADVENTURES

"Oh, I don't know if we believe you, Kocka! If we let you go, you'll just be right back to try to steal the princess again! I could turn these dogs loose on you, or we could make a pact with each other. You think we're not able to protect the princess now? We've proved we are fully capable of protecting her. She is the key to all of our lives, so we should work together in protecting her."

Solace crawled up on the tree and stood beside me. "Let's all make a pact with the princess to serve and protect her as long as she reigns."

Kocka said, "I have faith that she is in good hands and will be protected. We will to be at her call if she is ever in need."

All the animals bowed their heads to Solace in unison.

"Now if you will allow us to leave, we will return to the city to inform all the animals there of our pact."

The animals cleared a way for the cats to go through. The cats disappeared in the forest.

I looked down at the old dog and said, "I didn't say you couldn't make sure they went back to the city!"

The old dog smiled and said, "Come on, boys! Let's push 'em back to the city!" The dogs took off behind the cats at full speed. Last time anyone saw them, they were chasing the cats at full speed through the woods.

"Think they'll honor their pact?" Solace asked.

"We'll be here if they ever come back," I said.

"Everyone, please come to the stream bank. We'll bring food and drink for all!" Mr. Mudar shouted.

Everyone walked toward the stream, laughing and kidding with each other. They just successfully guarded the grove for the second time. Solace and I walked with them, holding hands and talking to Squeaky.

"I'm glad no one else had to die for me," Solace said.

"You are special to all the animals now that they know you are the key to all this."

"I don't understand it, but I don't wanna find out what would happen if something happened to you. That's not the only reason though. I couldn't live without you in my life, Solace," I said.

"You won't have to," Solace answered.

"Would y'all shut up! All this mushy bullcrap!"

CHAPTER 26

Life in the Grove

All the animals and everyone from the grove showed up at the stream bank. Everyone brought fruits and vegetables and nuts.

I went over to Pesco and thanked him for getting Solace to the grove safely. The guardians were in the front, thanking everyone for protecting the grove. They told everyone who wasn't from the grove that they were welcome anytime. It had been a long-standing rule that everyone had to be born in the grove or had to earn their way to be considered a resident.

Life at the grove was pretty simple. Everyone had their responsibilities. There were gardeners, carpenters, and even animals to doctor on injuries. The guardians had their animals to protect the grove. No one really ever leaves the grove; there's no need to. The grove had been in my granddad's family for generations. The animals in the grove were from generations of animals that have lived there. They were just regular animals doing normal animal things till about fifty years ago.

A blue-eyed squirrel just showed up one day, and things changed. All of a sudden, all the animals could speak to each other and do things that humans do. The animals all thought it came from my farm. Every ten years or so, a blue-eyed squirrel would show up, and the animals would stay like they were.

The special power of the blue eyes had spread to all the animals around the grove. That was why everyone wanted to have Solace so they could ensure her safety.

PIBBY'S ADVENTURES

Though some of the animals still hunt other animals, most didn't anymore. They'd found ways of growing gardens and protecting wild fruit trees.

The animals couldn't interact with humans. The humans would still see and hear them as regular animals. Most of the animals now had always been the way they were now. Only a few left that remember how it was to be the other way. Mr. Mudar was one of them. He knew how much Solace meant to the grove and all animals around the grove.

The celebration at the stream was all laughs and hugs. The guardians stood up and hushed the crowd to speak. "We have discussed the plans for the princess from this day forward. After what has happened in the past few days, we think she should stay under guard twenty-four hours a day. We don't think being in a relationship is a good idea, and she'll have personal guard with her every time she leaves her home. Solace will not be allowed to leave the grove for any reason. This is what we've decided as the guardians of this grove."

Solace looked at me in disbelief. Most of the animals listening agreed with the guardians. I stood up and shouted, "She's not a prisoner and will not be treated like one! What kind of life is this for someone?"

"The grove depends on her safety. It must be this way!" the guardians shouted.

The celebration got really quiet all of the sudden. Solace's dad came over and grabbed her by the arm and led her away from my side. "It's for the best!" he said.

I started to grab Solace, but Squeaky grabbed me and said, "Later, we'll handle it later."

Sova came up and stood behind me, showing his support. The crowd started slowly heading back to their homes, leaving just me and all the ones who helped saved the grove. They all pledged their support for me if I ever needed them.

Pesco said, "You know how to find me, buddy!"

Still troubled over Solace's dad's decision, I didn't talk much. Squeaky said, "You can come stay at my house, being you don't have one of your own yet."

149

"Mr. Mudar told me that I could crash at his house till I decided what I wanted to do," I said. I made my way through the forest, thinking about what to do now. With all that happened in the last few weeks, I had totally forgotten where I came from. I couldn't believe I forgot all about my brother and the rest of my family.

A sudden sadness rushed over me that I couldn't shake. I wondered if they missed me, or was I dead in the human world? Did they forget me by now, or were they all grieving over me? The last thing in the world that I wanted to do was hurt my family.

I decided that tomorrow, I would go to the farm and watch my family for a while. I didn't know if it mattered anyway. I didn't know any way of returning.

CHAPTER 27

Pibby's Choice

I made it to Mr. Mudar's place just in time for some blueberry cobbler he had made. We sat down and ate till our bellies were slam full. Mr. Mudar knew I was probably missing home, so he sat me down and told me his story.

"I was a boy once, a long, long time ago. Just like you, I woke up one day as a small turtle on the edge of the stream. I lived on the same farm your grandparents live on except about a 150 years ago. I'm probably one of your kinfolk somewhere down the line. I wrestled with everything you're wrestling with right now in your mind. You ask yourself why and how did this happen to you. I've done some investigating on this matter and found out that there are animals all over this grove and surrounding forests that are just like you and me. They all seem to like this life better than the other choice. None of them say they would go back if they could. I also found that you can go back if you so desire."

My eyes turned to stare at Mr. Mudar. "It's true, Pibby. The princess could walk you back to the place that you entered and lead you back to your former life. That's the power she holds, and a lot of animals know this fact. The only thing is, if she does this, she returns to a normal animal. She'll never be like us ever again. Solace doesn't know of this power she has. That's the reason I stayed. I couldn't ask my friend to do this for me."

"What happen to your friend?" I asked.

151

"I married her, and we had a glorious life together even though she was a princess of the grove at one time. Oh, they guarded her and tried to keep her a secret, but we enjoyed our life together here in the grove. She just vanished one day, and the next blue-eyed princess showed up. Oh, we had over hundred years together, but I miss her still to this day. Pibby, so you see why I couldn't ask her to give up something so precious?"

I shook my head and said, "Yes, sir. I would never ask Solace to do that for me. It seems so unfair for her to have to give up so much to help someone."

"That's why I never mentioned it to my princess," Mudar said.

I told Mudar that I was going for a swim in his pond and think for a while. Mr. Mudar knew what I was feeling, so he let me go and be on my own for a while. I swam for a little while and heard someone come in to the front door of Mr. Mudar's home.

Solace appeared by the pond and ask if she could come in. I said, "Sure! What are you doing here? Isn't your dad gonna be mad that you're here?"

"What he doesn't know won't kill him! Dads always been this way. Don't let it get to you. You know how hardheaded I am." Solace laughed.

Solace and I talked and laughed for a couple hours. Finally, Solace asked, "Do you wanna go back home, Pibby? I know I can do that for you. I was listening to one of the guardians' meetings at my home. I'd give up anything for you, Pibby, but I really want you to stay with me in this life."

I said, "I would never ask you to do that for me. I do miss home though. Will you go with me tomorrow to watch my family from the trees around their house?"

"Pibby, are you asking me on a date?" Solace giggled.

"Well, I guess, I am!" I laughed. "I would be honored to go on a date with you, my princess."

Solace told me she would be here at sunrise to get me as she was leaving. She gave me a big wet kiss on the lips and went skipping toward home. I could hear Mr. Mudar laughing in the background.

"That girl is smitten over you, Pibby!"

"She is something else!" I answered.

The next morning, Solace knocked on the door and came in. Mr. Mudar had fruits and greens made up for breakfast. We all ate, and Solace and I grabbed a lunch Mr. Mudar had packed for us and left for the farm.

We walked through the forest holding hands and talking about all that happened in the last few months.

"We're lucky to be alive, you know!" Solace laughed.

"Yeah, you could be married to the emperor and living in the city!" I laughed back.

It took about two and a half hours to get to the edge of the farm.

"Let's get in that tree above the front door. You can see in the front window from there," I said.

After finding a good spot, we could see the whole living room area and anyone that would walk out of the house. After a while, my papa walked in to the living room and sat down after turning the TV on. I could see a lot of different faces my papa was making at the TV.

"Papa watching his soaps again. He loves watching this time every day." Solace could see the joy on my face, seeing my papa again. She didn't know exactly what I was talking about but loved seeing me so happy.

They watched him watch TV all the while laughing at the different faces he made while watching it. About that time, a little green car pulled up in the driveway, and my granny got out with a big bag of leftovers from the Dairy Queen she worked at. About that time, two little girls and a boy ran out to meet my granny.

My eyes teared up and said, "That's Tracy, my brother, and my two sisters, Chelle and Beth." I just watched how happy they were to see Granny Mae show up with all those different kinds of ice cream. They all went inside the house, and I could see them all in the living room, eating Dilly Bars.

Granny was getting on to my papa for not picking the butter beans today. "Nag, nag, nag," my papa would say to her. I wondered if they were already over me or was I ever there?

Solace could tell what I was thinking and said, "When you left that day, it reset their lives as if you were never there. They don't know you ever existed."

I was sad and kinda happy that they didn't have to live with something like that. Another car pulled up about that time, and my mom got out of the car. Tears ran down my face as she stopped and watched the butterflies play on some lantana nearby. My mom went around the yard smelling all the flowers in the yard.

My granny really loved purple petunias. She had them planted everywhere. My mom went in and grabbed a Dilly Bar and sat down with the kids and ate it, watching some show on the TV. "I bet they're watching *Gilligan's Island*!" I said. "We watched it every day before Mom got home."

We could see my granny shelling butter beans while sitting on the couch and my papa had a bowl doing the same thing. We sat and watched my family all day long as they played under a big old house and climbed all the trees in the yard.

Chinaberry fights broke out with the whole family till Beth got hit in the eye, and the chinaberry throwing stopped. Solace watched as I was lost in the memories of home and how it made me feel. My mom finally got all the kids in her car and drove away. I knew I may not ever see them again as my beautiful family disappeared around the curve. My papa and my granny went back to shelling butter beans and fussing about the garden more.

I looked at Solace and said, "Let's go."

We went back across the yard and entered the grove. Solace stopped me and said, "That's where you appeared, right?"

I looked over at the Mr. Pibb can by the old oak tree and said, "Yep!"

"I'll send you back to your family right now if you wanna go. I know you miss them dearly, Pibby. Let me help you get back to your life," Solace said.

I thought for a second and said, "My life is with you, Solace. They don't even know I ever existed. They can't miss something they never knew. I would miss you for the rest of my life." We hugged and started back down the trail toward home.

I felt better now that I knew that my family wasn't living with a heartache over me. I was at home with Solace and my new friends in the grove. I stopped Solace and said, "But we are gonna have to have more adventures. We can't just lie around this grove, doing nothing."

Solace said, "I couldn't agree more."

We made it back to Mr. Mudar's place and went for another swim. Squeaky showed up and joined us in the pond.

"We decided we have to have another adventure soon!" Solace shouted to Squeaky across the pond.

"Pibby and I have our responsibilities as guardians of the grove. It's an honor a lot of animals would love to have," Squeaky said.

"I'm really honored that they chose me, but I may back out and just explore the surrounding forests. There's life out there, let's go find it!" I shouted.

"We can't risk anything happening to Solace, and you know they'll never let her leave the grove."

"I'll do anything I want to do, Squeaky!" Solace shouted.

Squeaky just rolled his eyes and said, "Right!"

I said, "Tell your dad I want to meet with them tomorrow to discuss me leaving the guardianship. I don't wanna do the same thing every day till the day I die. I wanna spend time with all our new friends we've made."

Mr. Mudar walked in and invited us to the kitchen for some fresh vegetables from his garden.

*****

I showed up bright and early the next day at the guardians' three trees. All three guardians came out and perched on their usual places. They discussed my decision to leave the guardianship and the consequences of that happening.

"You'll have to pick a job in the grove that provides some service to the grove. If you're gonna live in the grove, you'll have to contribute in some way. If you choose to live outta of the grove, you can only enter with our permission. Everyone that lives in this grove will abide by these rules."

I told the guardians I'd have a decision by the next day. Squeaky asked me to follow him to the stream so he could show me something. We got to the stream, and our boat was sitting on the bank.

"Pesco brought it upstream and left it here. He said that we may need it one day."

"You ever wonder where the stream leads too?" I asked.

"I bet it ends in the ocean somewhere."

"Just think what an adventure that would be, Squeaky. It would be a very long trip, for sure, but it would be the time of our lives," I said. Squeaky nodded his head in agreement. "That's what I'm doing, Squeaky. I'm leaving soon to see where that stream leads."

Squeaky argued, saying, "You're just gonna take off with no plan? That doesn't make any sense. You've earned your place in the grove, why throw that away?"

We argued on the bank most of the day about my decision. I knew that Squeaky wouldn't come with me and didn't blame him. I knew that Squeaky's place was with his family. I figured I'd stay around till they make me leave. I wanted to spend all the time I could with Solace and Squeaky.

After arguing about my decision, the two friends worked on making the boat better for a long trip. We made it a sailboat by erecting a long tree in the middle and making a sail out of a piece of cloth leftover from the celebration.

Rain proofing the cabin was done by packing clay between the logs. Storage bins were built to store food for longer periods of time. A weapon storage bin was also built for bows and arrows. Pesco showed up in the middle of all the work being done.

"Someone taking a trip?"

"I am, I'm going to see where this stream ends," I answered.

"I often wondered that myself. How would you like some company?" Pesco asked.

"You really wanna come with me? Won't you miss home?" I asked.

"The stream is my home. I just haven't seen it all! I would count it as an honor to travel with you, buddy." Pesco laughed.

"Well, it's a plan. We'll leave in two days!"

PIBBY'S ADVENTURES

Pesco and I talked about the trip and how long we would travel each day. Squeaky spoke up and asked, "Let's say you find where it ends at the ocean, what is the plan then? Do you travel across the ocean?"

"We figure it out when we make it to the ocean!" I shouted. "That's how adventures start! Not knowing what's gonna happen tomorrow is the best part of an adventure!"

Pesco told me he'd be waiting here in two days and swam back to tell his sisters. Squeaky and I left the stream and headed back to Mr. Mudar's. Squeaky was quite all the way back. He didn't understand why his best friend was choosing to leave after all they've been through. He had waited all his life to make his dad proud of him. He knew his dad wanted this for him for a long time.

*****

Solace was waiting at Mudar's place when they got back. "Where have you been all day?" she asked.

"Pesco brought the boat to the bank, and we've been working on it," I said.

Squeaky brushed by her, saying nothing, and headed to the pond. "What's wrong with him?" she asked.

I filled Solace in on my plan to leave in two days. Solace looked at me in disbelief. "How could you do that to us, Pibby? Don't I mean anything to you?" Solace stormed out and slammed the door behind her.

I started to follow her out when Mr. Mudar grabbed his arm and said, "Let her go, son. You can talk to her when she calms down. Trust me on this!" He laughed. "This plan of yours sounds like something I wish I'd done when I was younger. Can you give up on her?"

"I can't live doing the same thing every day! Of course, I don't wanna leave all my friends here in the grove," I answered. "I'll come back from time to time."

Mr. Mudar said, "I wish I could go with you, young man, but my time has passed. My advice is to go and find your place in the world."

I walked back to the pond and cannonballed right by Squeaky. Squeaky grabbed me and held me underwater. We played in the pond till we heard Mr. Mudar call us for dinner. Solace was sitting at the table when we came in.

We all laughed and enjoyed dinner together, knowing this may be our last together. Mr. Mudar brought out a big bowl of butter beans and set it in front of me. I laughed and filled my plate, running it over. After dinner, I offered to walk Solace home. Solace said okay, and we left together.

I explained how I felt about her and how I couldn't live in the grove every day. Solace said, "That's okay because I'm coming with you! I can't live with all these restrictions on me. Not to mention, I can't live without you."

I hugged her and said, "You just made me the happiest squirrel in this grove! I was gonna ask you, but I didn't wanna put that pressure on you. We can't let your dad know. He'll never let you leave."

Solace agreed and promised to keep it quiet. Solace said that she would pack and try to get it to the boat the next day. We arrived at her home and hugged, saying good night. What they didn't know was Squeaky was following through the trees, listening to them.

Squeaky waited for me to leave and Solace to go in before coming down. Squeaky was torn on what to do. He couldn't let the princess of the grove leave. He also couldn't betray his friends. Squeaky walked in his home and went to bed, not sleeping a wink. He knew he had two days to make up his mind.

I walked back in Mr. Mudar's home with a big smile on my face.

"She's going with you, ain't she?" Mudar asked. I shook my head yes. "You know you have to protect her with your life! The whole animal kingdom will count on you doing just that. I'm happy for you, and it's been a pure pleasure knowing you. You'll be greatly missed around here."

I gave him a hug and went to lie down. I felt the weight of the world on my shoulders as I fell asleep. Solace went to sleep smiling from ear to ear, knowing she'd be rid of all this worry over her well-being.

PIBBY'S ADVENTURES

The next morning came with Solace's dad standing at the end of her bed. "It's never gonna happen! You will not leave this home any time soon. Squeaky told us of Pibby's plan to take you from the grove. He will be forced to leave the grove immediately!"

"After all he's done for you! He saved me more than once!" Solace went to leave home, but two guards stopped her at the door. "Really? A prisoner in my own home!" Solace shouted, running back to her room.

*****

I was on my way to tell the guardians my plan to leave the grove. When I arrived, I was surrounded by the guardians' guards. I looked up at the guardians and asked, "What's going on!"

"You're being removed from the grove for planning to kidnap the princess. You will be asked to leave immediately!" Solace's dad shouted. "We will always be grateful to you for saving our princess and bringing her back to the grove. After hearing of your plans to leave with her, we decided it best for you to leave the grove."

"I want to talk to Solace!" I demanded.

"We have made our decision. You must leave now!"

"Solace!" I shouted. I didn't see her anywhere.

"Guards, escort him to the boat and make sure he leaves the grove! From this point on, you will be considered a threat to the princess!"

The guards pushed me in the direction of the stream. I hung my head and walked toward the boat. Squeaky watched it all from a tree above. He was heartbroken over reporting their plans to the guardians.

Meanwhile, Solace was locked in her room, and guards were posted at her door.

*****

Squeaky climbed down to talk to his dad. "You could've at least let him say goodbye to his friends!"

159

"Son, you will learn in the guardianship, you will have no friends. You can't let your guard down! The job of a guardian is to protect the grove for the rest of his life. That is his number one priority! Now get back to your job!" his dad shouted.

Squeaky walked away with his head hanging for what he did to his friends.

*****

I was made to board my boat, and they pushed it off the bank, and I was on my way downstream. The guards followed on the bank till I was out of the grove. I took an arrow and hit the water three times to alert Pesco of my early departure. Just like that, my friends were out of my life. Solace was gone forever.

I had lost both my families now. I didn't have a place in either family anymore. My mind was all over the place. Should I have fought for her, or did I do the right thing? She was safer there, and all her family was there.

I wasn't angry with Squeaky. He was doing his job that he was so proud of. Squeaky would be sorely missed by me though. He was like the brother I had back at the farm, always having my back no matter what. Solace would never leave my mind for the rest of my life.

I knew I had to work on accepting on what just happen, but it was gonna take a long time to get over. The stream was running faster than usual because of the rain from upstream. What everyone was calling a stream was actually a river. I knew the name from when my grandparents would take me fishing in it, Ogeechee River, though I didn't know where it ended up because we hardly ever traveled anywhere. That's all about to change though because I was bound and determined to found out.

Pesco showed up about an hour after they forced me to leave. I explained why I had to leave and all about Solace and Squeaky. Pesco said that he was sorry and wish things could've turned out better for me. I thanked him for coming and keeping me company on my journey.

PIBBY'S ADVENTURES

Pesco talked for two hours straight about what the ocean must look like. I told him stories of some movies I saw with big sharks and all other kinds of animals in the ocean. "I've even heard of some famous fish called Moby Dick! Everybody knows of this whale! They even wrote books about him," I said.

"They're gonna write books of our adventures one day, I bet! I'll be as famous as this Moby Dick!" Pesco shouted out loud.

"I think you're right, Pesco, the great adventures of Pesco and Pibby! Heroes of the sea!"

We both laughed and started telling stories of what kind of adventures we wanna experience. I was relieved that I wasn't alone anymore. It would keep my mind off Solace.

Pesco swam with his back up against the bottom of the boat so I could relax and sit while Pesco steered it. We talked till it turned dark and pulled over and rested for a while.

*****

Squeaky left to go on his rounds with his father's words running through his head—about this being his job for the rest of his life. *Was Pibby right?* Did he want to do this every day of his life? What kind of life would that be? I had been gone for a day, and it already seemed like a year to him. Adventures sounded so good to him compared to doing this all day every day.

Squeaky knew who to talk to about all this. He headed to Mr. Mudar's place to get some advice.

*****

Solace was pacing back and forth in her room, yelling for them to let her out. She didn't sleep at all the night before, thinking of me. She knew her dad didn't give me a choice. I had to leave her here. Solace couldn't cry because she was too mad at her father. Living like this was not an option for her in her mind. She was gonna find a way to me no matter what it took.

After a little while, her dad came and let her out. He told her not to leave the sight of the guard he had posted to her. "I'm going to Mr. Mudar's, so he better be willing to walk then!" She knew Squeaky would be there, feeling guilty of what he did.

The guard kept up with Solace's every step. Solace didn't know what she was gonna say to Squeaky, but he wasn't gonna like it. She couldn't believe he would betray his friends like that. *Living in a guardian's house isn't easy, but that doesn't give you any right to turn in your friends!* she thought to herself.

When she got to Mudar's house, she didn't even knock. She just went straight in and pointed at Squeaky and said, "How dare you! Why, Squeaky! We're your friends!"

Squeaky sat at the table with his head hung. Mr. Mudar told Solace to sit down and listen. "Squeaky was doing his job. You know how much pressure they put on you living there! If he hadn't done what he did, the whole grove would've blamed him for your disappearance. Now you must accept what has happened and move on with your lives!"

"Pibby is gone and not coming back!" Solace finally let her tears flow and walked back to the pond.

Squeaky told Mudar, "I'm gonna go see if I can make things right with her. I can't stand her being mad at me." Squeaky walked back to the pond where Solace was sitting with her head on her knees, crying.

"I'm sorry I hurt you, Solace, but I've got some good news to tell you."

"What could you possibly tell me that was good?" she shouted.

"I'm leaving to join Pibby, and I want you to come with me."

Solace looked up and said, "When!"

"Slow down, we've got to be smart about this. If we get caught, they'll lock you up for good! First of all, we can't tell a soul about it. Not even Mr. Mudar," he whispered.

Solace hugged his neck and said, "Just let me know what you plan, and I'll do it! Oh yeah, I have a guard that follows me 24-7."

"Let me think of a plan and get with you here tomorrow. Solace, you got to play the part. Don't go around all happy-go-lucky. They'll know something's up."

PIBBY'S ADVENTURES

Solace agreed and pretended she was still crying as she left Mr. Mudar's place. She'd get better with time, he told Squeaky. Time heals or makes you forget a lot of things. The pain never goes completely away, but it dulls a little.

Squeaky thanked Mr. Mudar for all his advice and headed back to his rounds to think about his Pibby on the stream. He knew he had to move pretty fast. How could he get somewhere fast? "I've got it!" he shouted out loud. "Sova! He could fly Solace and me to the boat in no time. I got to leave early in the morning to talk to Sova and make it back before dark." He didn't wanna raise any suspicions.

Squeaky finished his rounds and went to find Solace and tell her his plans. Solace was outside sitting in the sun when Squeaky arrived. The guard was sitting in the tree not far away, eating. Squeaky went and sat by Solace and told her of his plans to ask Sova to fly them to the boat.

She whispered that she still had the vest that Mr. Lapin had made them in her room. Squeaky told her to pack her stuff and hide it somewhere and to be ready at a moment's notice and that he would fill her in when he got back tomorrow.

Squeaky went home and packed some stuff to take to the bank of the stream. He knew he would have one chance at getting away with Solace, so he had to be careful. After thinking about leaving his dad and life behind, he wasn't as sad as he thought he should be. Squeaky guessed that showed that he wasn't as happy as he thought he was at being a guardian. He lay down to rest and fell asleep.

Squeaky slept through the night and was awake before the sun rose. He decided to go ahead and head to Sova's forest. Sneaking out of his house was easy because his room was near the front door. Leaving the tree, Squeaky looked back and thought this could be the last time he would see his home. After standing there for a second, he turned and left for Sova's.

*****

Solace woke up and ate breakfast with her dad. He told her he was sorry that he sent me away, but it was for her own good. Her dad

163

continued to tell her how important she was to the animals in the forest. Solace told her dad she understood and that she loved him. She knew she would miss him when she left. All her stuff was packed and ready. All she had to do was get it to the stream bank.

After breakfast, her dad left to make his rounds in the grove, but the guard was still waiting at the bottom of the tree. Solace snuck out the door and crawled up the tree with all her stuff in a sack on her back. She went as high as she could and jumped to the next tree. Three trees later, and she was free of the guard. She stayed in the trees for a while to be sure she was far enough from her home before coming down.

An hour later, she was at the bank of the stream. She hung her stuff in a tree above the stream and headed home. When she got home, she walked up to the guard and asked where he was this morning and that she was gonna report to her dad about his tardiness.

"I'm going to Mr. Mudar's place if you wanna do your job for a change."

*****

Squeaky made his way to the edge of the grove by the time the sun rose. He knew the trail he was taking would take him through where Mr. Lapin lived. Hoping he would have time to stop and visit, he walked a little faster as he entered the open field. It would take him about two hours to reach the falls and two more to reach Sova's forest. So he figured he would have plenty of time, especially if Sova flies him back.

His thoughts were on me and how far I made it downstream. He hoped I hadn't had to face any dangers without him to be there to help me. Squeaky arrived at the falls, and it was full of animals that were glad to see him.

Jacare the gator asked about me and Solace and where we were. Squeaky told all of them what their plans were and where I was at the moment. They all wished him the best and told him if they ever needed them to let them know. Squeaky left the lake and headed to Mr. Lapin.

PIBBY'S ADVENTURES

Mr. Lapin was working in his shop when he arrived. They hugged, and Squeaky filled him with all the plans of leaving the grove. Mr. Lapin said that he understood and might have something to help them. He showed Squeaky a basket with two handles for Sova to grasp and haul three or four animals at a time. Lapin told Squeaky to stop by on the way back and have Sova pick it up.

They talked for a while and said their goodbyes, and Squeaky was on his way. It wasn't long till Squeaky reached the forest's edge. He wasted no time in calling out for Sova and heading inside the forest. Sova appeared after an hour or so and was glad to see Squeaky.

"It's been boring around here since y'all been gone. What did I do to deserve this honor?" Sova asked.

Squeaky told him of his plan and asked if he would help him and Solace. Sova said he would be honored to help. "I don't have a vest, but Mr. Lapin said he would have something we could use if we would stop by. I think it's some kinda basket to carry more at one time. We got to hurry to be able to catch Pibby," Squeaky said.

"Well, let's get going, bud!" Sova said as he grabbed Squeaky and took off through the trees. Sova was really happy to be back with friends, especially Squeaky. The two of them weren't really close at the beginning.

He flew as fast as he could to Lapin's place. Sova flew over a pond and dipped down and dragged Squeaky through the water. Squeaky laughed, saying, "You trying to tell me something?"

"Everyone needs a bath!" Sova shouted.

"I still have my bow with me, bird!"

They both laughed as they headed to Lapin's place.

*****

Solace made it to Mr. Mudar's place and made the guard stay outside. She knew she shouldn't tell him, but she needed someone to talk to her dad after she left. Solace told Mudar about their plans to leave and the things she wanted him to tell her dad. Mr. Mudar understood because of what he went through with his wife. He made her promise to be safe and that he would talk to her dad.

Solace hugged him and said, "Thank you for all the advice and good food." She headed back home to wait on Squeaky.

*****

Sova and Squeaky reached Lapin's place, and he had the basket ready for them. It had two handles and plenty room for two people and their supplies. They said their goodbyes, and Squeaky climbed in, and they were on their way. The plan was for Sova to wait at the stream bank till morning. Squeaky would meet Solace in the forest behind their home and come to Sova.

They arrived to the bank of the stream late in the evening. Squeaky told Sova he'd be back early in the morning with Solace.

"You know I can see to fly at night! I say we leave in the cover of darkness, it'll be safer," Sova said.

Squeaky thought for a minute and said, "Okay, we'll be back in a little while."

Sova said okay and flew up to a tree to rest awhile. Squeaky made it home around the same time he usually does every day. Solace was waiting out in front of their homes for him. They walked away from where her guard could hear her, and Squeaky told her they were leaving tonight. "You think you can get out without waking your dad?" Squeaky asked.

"Yeah, I do it all the time, but the guard may be a problem. I fooled him early today. I may not be able to do it again."

"I'll take care of the guard," Squeaky said.

"Don't shoot him!" Solace said.

"I'm not gonna shoot him. You just meet me in the trees behind your home in a couple hours." Squeaky scoffed at her.

"Whatever! I'll be there!" she whispered while walking away.

Squeaky went up to his home to eat with his dad, maybe for the last time. They talked and laughed while they ate their bellies full. Solace did about the same with her dad and went to her room. Then two hours went by, and Squeaky was already standing behind Solace's guard in the woods. He took his bow and whacked the guard behind the head, and he fell to the ground.

PIBBY'S ADVENTURES

Solace climbed down and walked up to the guard and said, "I told you not to kill him!"

"He's not dead. Come on, let's go before he comes to," Squeaky ordered.

They arrived at the stream, and Sova was waiting for them. "Y'all ready to find Pibby?"

"Yes!" they both shouted. They climbed in, and they were off headed downstream.

CHAPTER 28

The Reunion

I woke up early the next morning, ready to get back on the water.

Pesco popped his head up and said, "Let's go. We're burning daylight!"

We slid the boat in the stream, and we were off. The day was perfect, and the waters were calm. I ate while Pesco steered the boat from underneath. The river started to widen out and flowed a little faster now. I thought about my friends back home while I ate. I wondered what they were doing without me creating trouble in the grove. I told myself I would visit them again one day, no matter what the guardians had said.

Pesco sunk down and let the boat drift on its own for a while. I grabbed the rudder and steered. We came upon a bunch of animals wading on the bank of the river. As we went by, all the animals shouted, "Where are you headed?"

I steered the boat over to the bank and said, "We're headed to wherever this river takes us!"

They all laughed and said, "Everyone knows it ends at the ocean. There are things in that ocean that eat little things like you! That little boat won't make it in that water either."

I ignored them, saying, "Well, I'm gonna find out on my own!" I pushed off.

They waved, saying, "Good luck, you'll need it!"

PIBBY'S ADVENTURES

Pesco surfaced beside the boat and told me the water was getting a little salty now. "We must be getting close!"

About that time, three dolphins surfaced on the other side, telling them there was danger up ahead for them.

"Sharks!" they shouted.

I remembered TV shows where sharks ate anything they saw. Pesco told me he couldn't go any farther because of the salt water. "I'm sorry, buddy, but this is where I leave your adventure!"

We said our goodbyes, and Pesco watched as I floated down the river. I was sad to see Pesco go and felt really alone now. I had to worry about the danger at hand right now. The first shark I encountered just swam up and looked at me. The second one bumped my little boat and swam off. I knew they could swallow the whole boat if they chose too.

I steered the boat over to the nearest sandbar and pulled the boat safely on to it. The shark circled the island surfacing, saying, "You know the water rises here, and soon you'll have no choice to come back in!"

I knew nothing about tides, but the water did seem to be ever so slightly. The sandbar was in the middle of the river, so there was no way I could make it to the bank. I tried to figure out a way to get to the bank, but it was no use. The sharks would get me the moment I got in the water.

The water had risen to my feet now and had no signs of stopping. I climbed on top of the boat and started waving at the birds that were flying all around. "Please help me!" I shouted.

One seagull finally noticed me and flew down to me. "What was that you said, squirrel?"

"Help me get to the bank. These sharks are gonna eat me if I stay out here!" I shouted.

"That's what we're counting on. They eat you, and we pick up the pieces!" The seagull laughed.

"I've got a whole bag of fruits and nuts. Y'all can have them all!"

"Well, okay, show me the food!"

I pulled out the sack of food, and the seagull flew down and grabbed the bag. I grabbed the bag, and the seagull picked me and the bag in the air. The seagull did a few loops and twist to shake me off, but it didn't work. I climbed to the top of the bag, pulled my sword, and poked the seagull, saying, "Take me to the bank, or we both get eaten by the sharks!"

The seagull turned toward the bank and dropped me and the bag safely on the bank and flew away. After calming down, I found a shelter in an old oak tree nearby. I dragged the bag inside for safe-keeping and settled in for the night.

This adventure sure started off with a *bang*! I thought to myself, *I might have bitten off more than I can chew. Should I keep going or turn back now?* I drifted off to sleep, wondering what to do next.

*****

Sova flew most of the night while Solace and Squeaky slept in the basket below. He finally landed and hung the basket on a limb and rested above it. They were about a day from where I was. Morning came and Sova grabbed the basket and took off downstream again, looking for any signs of me.

Solace and Squeaky were doing the same, looking over the sides of the basket.

*****

I slept in late because I didn't know what to do next. My boat was gone, and all I knew to do was follow the river by land. After climbing down the old oak, I found a path by the river that looked like it had been used a lot. I threw my bag over my shoulder and started walking.

By the end of the day, Sova had spotted my boat turned upside down in the middle of the sandbar where I left it. Turned out, the water didn't come up much more after I left. Sova swooped down and landed on the sandbar. Squeaky jumped out and ran over to the boat.

After looking all around it, he shouted, "Nothing here!"

PIBBY'S ADVENTURES

"Oh my goodness! You think he drowned or was eaten by something!" Solace cried out.

"Don't jump to conclusions!" Squeaky barked back.

About that time, a shark surfaced and laughed. "You have a lucky little friend. He nearly escaped us eating him by hitching a ride to the bank over there."

Squeaky drew his bow and barely missed hitting the shark dead in the eyes. Sova grabbed the basket, and after they jumped in, he flew to the nearby bank. Squeaky and Solace jumped out while Sova flew ahead to see if he could locate me.

Squeaky picked up my trail, and they started following my footsteps. "What kinda fish was that back there? I've never seen one that would eat squirrels!" Solace asked.

"I don't know, but traveling by water is not an option anymore. Did you see all those birds flying around? This place is awesome!" Squeaky shouted.

"Awesome? This place is dangerous! Exactly why you like it, right?" Solace said.

*****

I caught a shadow of a big bird flying overhead. My instincts made me dive into a safe place so it couldn't see me. Sova swooped down and landed right in front of me.

"You've got to hide better than that, little squirrel!" he said in a deep voice.

I jumped out with sword drawn and ready for a battle. "Sova! What are you doing here?" I shouted.

"Well, looking for you, of course. I heard you were going on a little adventure and figured you would want some company! Oh, by the way, I've got two more surprises for you! Turn around!" Sova said.

I turned around, and Solace almost knocked me over by jumping on my arms at full speed. I couldn't believe my eyes.

Squeaky came over and put his arm around me and said, "You didn't think you could leave us behind, did you?"

I couldn't get the words to come out. "But how?"

"Well, let's just say, there's some mad fathers back at the grove right about now!" Solace said.

We all sat around and talked about the last two days and the close calls they had.

Sova spoke up and said, "Where are we going next?"

"You mean you're staying with us?" Solace asked.

"I can't think of any place that I'd rather be! And just think of the adventure that lies ahead for us!"

"Well, that settles it! It's the four of us! We'll see where this river ends and what lies beyond together!" I shouted.

The three of them climbed in the basket, and Sova flew off in the sunset toward the coast.

ABOUT THE AUTHOR

Keith has seven grandkids and has four kids of his own. He believes kids need to get back to the books and exercise their imagination more.

Growing up on a small Georgia farm, he and his brother had made up imaginary games and explored the woods around their granddad's farm. He claims his childhood was the best even without having as much as most of the other kids. Keith says, "Imagination can take you to any place in God's great universe!"

Printed in the USA
CPSIA information can be obtained
at www.ICGtesting.com
LVHW050832290524
781182LV00002B/279